SMALL TOWN TROUBLE

R.J. Amos

1

The carefully curated alarm music on Mel's phone always sounded perfectly reasonable the night before but somehow modulated into shrieking birds by the next morning. She'd tried all the possible alarms but none made Monday mornings any more palatable. Maybe it was something about getting up while it was still dark.

She checked her phone for urgent messages or emails but apart from the looming meeting with Sharon there was nothing. And that was fine. The meeting with Sharon, the managing director, was enough by itself. A meeting with the big boss meant nothing but trouble.

'What sort of trouble though?' she asked herself for the fifty thousandth time that weekend. 'And what sort of boss drops that bomb on you just before you leave work on Friday?'

Clothes shrugged on, and hair tied back, Mel headed out for her morning jog. The sky was just beginning to lighten, but not by much. There was too much cloud cover to get even a hint of pink this morning, not that she could have seen it over the high-rise buildings. All the lights were against her too; she spent more time jogging on the spot waiting for lights to change than she did actually moving forward. And when she felt the first spit of rain on her face she gave it all up as a bad joke and headed back to the apartment for a long hot shower. If this was a foretelling of the week ahead she would need all the comfort a shower could give.

Mel worked at Thompson's, a medium-sized company that took produce from the farmers, packaged it, and delivered it throughout the country to the big supermarket chains. Thompson's was all about fruit and vegetables, fresh air and the country life, if you believed its advertising, but in reality the country had not been any part of Mel's working life. She worked in the Melbourne office. The office took up three floors of a skyscraper in the inner city. She was working her way up the ladder, and everyone in her working group knew it. She was on her way to be CEO, like her father, the owner of Thompson's. But days like this made her wonder just how long that was going to take, and just how much work she would need to put in.

It was definitely that kind of morning. The long hot shower was too long, as it turned out. One sniff of the milk carton showed her that she would have to stop at the café on the way to the station to get her life-giving coffee. And then she dashed down the subway stairs only to see the train pulling out just as she arrived on the platform. Why couldn't it have been two minutes late like it normally was?

Checking her phone again while she waited for the next train (that was, incidentally, running two minutes late), there was an email from Sharon to say that the meeting had been moved forward half an hour, giving her about five minutes from when she'd get off the train to be in her office, up to speed on everything, and ready to defend herself to the big boss. Whatever she was defending herself for.

But once in the train, she was grateful for the five minutes she'd had on the platform to gulp her coffee. It would have been impossible to drink it on the train, squashed as she was between a smelly armpit and a backpack that was holding something entirely made up of sharp corners.

The dash from the station to the office through the rain left her skirt splashed with mud from the traffic and she needn't have bothered with the precious minutes spent blowdrying her hair.

Altogether it wasn't an auspicious start to the week.

All things considered, it was something of a triumph to only be two minutes late knocking on Sharon's door for the meeting.

Mel always hated this office. It was probably because it reminded her so much of her father's. Big black desk, big picture windows overlooking the city, the feeling of impending doom as you walked through the door to get more bad news, the feeling of insignificance as you sat ill at ease in the straight-backed chair and wondered which of your failings was going to be painted in technicolour today.

'I was wondering when you'd show up,' said Sharon, gesturing to the chair in front of the desk. 'You're going to have to get a bit more punctual in your new position, I'm sure.'

New position? Maybe this wasn't a bad-news meeting after all. Mel sat with her head held high and back straight, and waited for some clarification.

'I've brought you here this morning to offer you a more managerial placement. Would you be interested?'

Managerial? That sounded ... hang on ... there had to be a catch.

'I'm interested,' Mel said cautiously, 'could I have more information?'

'Certainly.' Sharon crossed her legs and sat back to tell the story. 'As you know, the board has been concerned about our relationship with our primary producers. There have been issues, situations caused by the management being centralised and, shall we say, losing touch with the farmers. The issues are becoming more pronounced as we work to incorporate the changes that will lead to the farms being more energy efficient, and more environmentally friendly. There has been some resistance. The answer to that issue is to send managers out into the field, as it were.' Sharon paused so that Mel could acknowledge the pun with a weak smile. 'You are the first person chosen to fill this position. I am here to offer you a management position in Lillyford, working to integrate environmental footprint changes. Lillyford is a town close to several of our major farms and you would be the liaison between us here in the city, and the producers out there.'

'Lillyford! But that's ... that's in the middle of nowhere.' Mel blinked. She had worked hard to rise through the ranks of Thompson's. She had been sure that a promotion was just around the corner. She had big dreams of being CEO, if not of this place, then of somewhere similar. And now, Lillyford. A town she only knew existed because she had seen it on delivery orders and office paperwork. A tiny place, right in the middle of Tasmania. The state of Tasmania was a place she had never wanted to go to. Not even for holidays. She was a city girl. She had dreams of leaving Melbourne to go to New York or London. Not this, this was the wrong way. What had she done to be sent out to the country? This had to be a punishment for something. Sharon must want to get rid of her.

'In the middle of the farms, yes.' Sharon was unperturbed. She leafed through some papers on her desk and found a file. 'You would be looking after Hopwoods, Lingholm, Northfield …'

'What's this about, Sharon?' Mel forgot her professional attitude, put both fists on the desk and leaned forward. 'What have I done to be kicked out like this?'

Sharon looked Mel in the eye, 'Kicked out? This is a promotion to a managerial position.'

'Is there an increase in salary?'

Sharon looked at the desk again, 'Not as such, no. But I'm sure you'll find your expenses are less in a smaller town. And you have to appreciate we are investing in an office …'

'Kicked out.' Mel stood up. 'My whole career would be buried by this move. I'd lose my lease, I'd lose touch with what was happening here in the hub. No. No way.' And what would her father think of this? He owned Thompson's, and while he was completely hands-off when it came to Mel, preferring his daughter to work her way up with no special treatment, even he would be unhappy with this turn of affairs, she was sure. He wouldn't want her to be shut down like this.

Sharon leant back comfortably in her chair, easily meeting Mel's eyes.

'Melody, it doesn't matter what you think the reason is. The fact of the matter is that I am offering you this position in Lillyford. It is a position of some significance and responsibility. I think you'll find that Lillyford is a new challenge, a change that you need. Think it over, and get back to me.'

Mel grimaced at the use of her full name. That was another reason she didn't like to meet with Sharon.

'I don't need to think. You can offer this to someone else. Try Tom. I'm sure he'd take it. I'm not interested.'

Sharon frowned slightly and nodded, looking less sure than she had for the whole meeting. She half reached out her hand, but Mel was firm. She stood, nodded her goodbye to Sharon, and left the office. She'd been clear. There was nothing Sharon could offer her that would make her want that job.

She hoped it *would* be offered to Tom. It would get him out of the office. He was so slimy, that man. She wondered whether he was behind this, whether it was his aim to get her out of the way so that he could get the promotion she was working for. You really had to watch your back, didn't you?

Picking up her bag, Mel grabbed her friend Evie by the arm.

'Evie, we're going for coffee.'

'But …' Evie gestured at her computer.

'No buts. I need coffee now, and I need you. I'll help you finish anything you're working on but we need to go now.'

'Alright, if that's the way it is.' Evie grabbed her bag and stood up in one smooth movement. 'I'm always up for a coffee.'

The girls made their way through the cubicle maze to the door and down the stairs. The look on Mel's face made their co-workers duck out of her way and then exchange significant glances as she passed. Once they got to the pavement Mel sped up even more.

'Mel, slow down.' Evie whinged. 'I can't keep up. I've got new shoes on and I'm going to break an ankle at this pace.'

'Oh, sorry, I didn't even realise I was going fast. I'm just so angry.'

She waited, arms crossed, unconsciously tapping her fingers. Evie strolled maddeningly slowly, eventually catching up to the impatient Mel.

'Do you like them?'

'What?'

'My shoes! Aren't they gorgeous? Found them in a bargain bin on Saturday on my way to get groceries. I couldn't resist.'

Mel looked at Evie. She really was a picture, from her blonde Marilyn Monroe bob through her cherry-red dress with white polka dots to the matching shoes with the two-inch heels. But Evie needed to know, especially today, there was more to life than shoes.

'They're very nice.' Mel's voice was flat. 'And you never can resist.'

'But these, they're so gorgeous.' Evie was a little pouty.

'Sorry Evie.' Mel started walking again but at a slower pace this time. 'I just have more important things on my mind right now.'

'More important than shoes?'

Mel laughed, 'Yes, there are a few more important things than shoes out there. I know you find that hard to believe but wait until I tell you this news.'

'Out with it then.'

'Not until I get a coffee. This is going to need some unpacking.'

The girls found their favourite booth at the back of their usual store, and ordered their coffees—flat white for Mel, mocha with two sugars for Evie. Mel prepared to tell her story. Evie was the office gossip, but she was also Mel's oldest friend, and the person who brightened her day. Evie's presence at the neighbouring desk was sometimes the only thing that got her into the office on a Monday morning.

'OK, here's the news. She wanted to transfer me.'

'A promotion?'

'Nope. A demotion if you ask me. She wanted me to work in Lillyford. Lillyford!'

'Lillyford? But that's in Tasmania. I mean, you'd have to move. You can't commute from here, you need to fly. Or worse, take the ferry.'

'Exactly. That's why I turned her down.' Mel took a refreshing sip of her coffee.

'Turned her down?' Evie was wide-eyed.

'It would be career suicide. I would lose my apartment. I would lose my place in the office. And who would have employed me with months or years lost working out in the middle of nowhere? Who would take me seriously?'

'Surely it wouldn't be that bad. You've always said that you could do a better job if you were given more control. Maybe you can use this opportunity to prove it.'

'More control? Over what? I want to manage the office here, not fields of cabbages. I said no. They can give it to Slimy Tom. Get him out of the office.'

'You've never liked him, have you?' Evie sat back in her seat and took a sip of her sweet drink.

Mel shook her head. 'He's never liked me. He's a horrible man.'

'But a bit dishy, you've got to admit that.' Evie looked at Mel slyly.

'Evie, you and men. I don't have to admit that. What's inside shows on the outside. He's a nasty piece of work.'

'He's never been a problem for me. You and he just got off on the wrong foot.'

Mel lifted her cup to her lips and thought about it.

'You could be right. But I'm pretty sure he's been reporting every one of my little slip-ups to Sharon. He's been trying to get promoted to my position for ages. I'm sure he'll be happy to take the job if it's given to him as a promotion. He'll probably wangle a pay rise too.'

Evie shook her head.

'There wasn't a pay rise?'

'Nope. Just an assurance that life would be cheaper there. Not convinced. But anyway, I've said no.'

The two girls chatted and Mel felt her blood pressure falling. Eventually she drained the last of her coffee. 'Thanks for the chat Evie. I guess now I've turned Sharon down I'm going to have to work doubly hard to get anywhere in this place. But I'm sure I've done the right thing.'

'Of course you have.'

'And hopefully I've heard the last of this. I can't believe that Sharon thought I'd even think about it.'

The girls pulled themselves out of the booth.

'But Mel, more importantly, don't you think these are the most gorgeous shoes you've ever seen? You didn't really look at them before. Look how strappy they are, and red, too!'

Mel laughed. She felt much better.

'Yes, Evie, they are the most gorgeous shoes I've ever seen. Happy?'

Mel and Evie headed back to work, Mel happy to put this day and all thoughts of Lillyford behind her.

2

The next Monday turned out to be almost a carbon copy of the week before. Once again, last thing on Friday Mel had been told to go to Sharon's office first thing Monday. Once again she'd spent the weekend worrying about what that meant for her. Was she losing her job?

Would she have to pull the Dad card? That was the question. But how embarrassing if she couldn't even hold down a job at her own father's business. She would almost prefer to lose the job altogether and pick up a new one somewhere. Maybe she *would* prefer that. But the option of looking for a new job was daunting. Especially after getting fired. Where would she find anyone willing to give her a reference? So maybe she would have to go with whatever Sharon said. Maybe Lillyford was the only option. But Lillyford! Surely she could be more valuable to the company somewhere else? Maybe she would just need to change departments. She had argued with herself over and over again throughout the whole weekend.

On Sunday night she tossed and turned. Every time she closed her eyes she saw job application forms dancing in front of her eyeballs. Or long benefit queues. Or … She couldn't lose her job. That would be crazy. She wasn't prepared.

She felt like she'd had a whole thirty straight minutes of sleep when the screeching alarm went off. She decided to grab a few more minutes instead of going for her regular jog. That of course meant that she fell deeply asleep and when she woke up she looked at her phone and found she had a mere five minutes left to get out of the house.

She slapped on skirt and shoes, deciding to forgo stockings to save time. She pulled her hair back in a messy bun as she raced down the stairs to the train platform. If she was lucky she could slap on some makeup during her morning break but right now she just had to get to the office.

The train pulled up as she ran onto the platform and she turned up at the office, harried and out of breath, but on time.

Once again, Mel faced the closed office door. But her night's sleep (or lack thereof) had decided her. She was not going to Lillyford, for sure. There was nothing Sharon could say that would convince her. There was no reward that she wanted. But she wasn't leaving the company either. They couldn't threaten her, her father would have words to say if she was sacked for something as small as this. She would play the Dad card if she needed to.

'Shoulders back, chin up,' she said to herself. 'You know who you are, act like it.' And she knocked on the door.

The voice saying, 'Come in,' was not Sharon's voice, but it was a voice Mel recognised only too well and she couldn't keep the shock off her face as she stepped in quickly and shut the door behind her.

'Good morning, Melody.' Her father gestured at the chair in front of him, acting like this was an everyday occurrence. But it was far from that.

'Good morning, Father, I didn't expect to see you here.'

Mel sat stiffly, and waited for some clarification.

'It's my company. I think I can be wherever I want to be.'

Mel decided not to mention that she had never seen him in her department before, that he had been so determined that she would work her way up without any help from the boss, without any preferential treatment, that she had seen him less since she started work for Thompson's than she had before. If that were possible.

'If you can bear to talk with your father for a few minutes, I'd like to discuss something with you.'

Mel sighed. Why did he have to be so defensive?

'Of course I'd be happy to talk with you, Father. I'm just a bit confused as to why we are here, and why all the secrecy? Why didn't you tell me we were meeting? I thought I was meeting with Sharon. I thought this was some disciplinary hearing. I've been worried all weekend.'

He looked down at the desk, having the grace to appear slightly embarrassed.

'I could have done this differently I suppose, but there actually is a need for secrecy. In fact, I have tried already—I was hoping that you'd take the offer from Sharon and I could fill you in later, but … well.'

'You want me to go to Lillyford?'

'Yes, I want you to go to Lillyford.'

'Why? Why do you want me out of the city? Do you want to bury my career in some little out of the way town? Have I caused you any problems? I've all but buried our relationship. No one here knows I'm your daughter except Evie. And she's been keeping mum about it. I'm sure she's almost forgotten. And I'm working just as hard as anyone else, harder than most, I think. What have I done wrong?'

Mel's father rubbed his hands on his trouser legs. He pushed the chair back from the desk and sat forward with his hands on his knees.

'Nothing. You've done nothing wrong. It's not like that at all, Melody. Surely …' he sighed and adjusted his chair again. 'This is what it is. I don't want to alarm you but I have an assignment that requires some delicacy and I think that you are the best person to fill it.'

'Alarm me?' said Mel. And then incredulously, 'A delicate assignment in Lillyford?'

'Indeed. In Lillyford. Where do I start?' He looked through a few of the papers on the desk, then took a breath and started again. 'There have been some … anomalies. Some gaps in reports. Some judicious hiding of something. I can't be more clear. If I knew what was going on I wouldn't have to be meeting with you. Of course I'll give you all the information we have. But it's not much.'

'This isn't making much sense, Father.'

'That's what I'm telling you. Just hear me out. There are anomalies, as I say, in the produce coming out of the Lillyford area. Some of the trucks have gone missing, or turned up late. Some of the weights and measures don't add up. It's being well hidden, but our audit last month turned up just enough questions to make me nervous. There may be nothing going on. But there may be something, and sitting here in Melbourne is not going to figure it out for me. I need someone to be on the ground to work out what's happening. I want you to be that someone.'

'You want to send me out to woop-woop to grub in the dirt with the farmers, to look for an "anomaly" that might not exist. How can this be good for me?'

Mr Thompson's face hardened. Mel knew that expression and before she could stop herself she checked the desk for the presence of a wooden spoon.

'We work in produce. The farmers, the growers, they are the reason we exist as a company. We should not think of ourselves as too good to go to them and see what's happening. If your attitude is like that, I should have sent you out there years ago when you started. You can't look down on the country.'

'I don't see you spending much time out there.'

'I'm not able to do that now, certainly, but when I started to build up this business ...'

'I know, I know, you were out there working in the fields, picking out the gravel by hand, heading to work in the snow, uphill both going to work and coming home ...'

Mel's father slammed his hand on the desk and stood up.

'Obviously you can't handle this responsibility! I will just have to find someone else. I thought I could trust you because you were my daughter, but I'm sure Tom will be able to do it. Or Senka, we don't have to go any further.'

Mel stood up too. 'I didn't say that. You've just thrown this at me and I haven't had any time to think. I have a life here, you know, I can't just throw it all away in an instant. I need a bit of time, at least, to figure this out. Just give me a few minutes.'

He nodded, sat back down and quietly shuffled papers. She sat in the straight-backed chair and chewed her lip. Why did she have to react like an angry teenager whenever they talked? And how would she live in Lillyford? She was a city girl, born and bred. What were country towns even like?

She got up and walked over to the window, the familiar layout of streets and buildings before her. How could she move from this to a little country town?

But Mel's father had known what he was doing. For all their inability to communicate and the amount of time they didn't see each other, Mel could see that her father knew his daughter. She knew that the threat of having Tom do the job was calculated on his part, not the off-hand comment that it appeared. He knew she would never let some upstart bloke from the office take a position of responsibility like this one.

She came back to the desk, and looked at her father. He sat silently, staring at the papers on the desk, his face unreadable, giving nothing away. He didn't look like he needed anyone's help. He sat there, the strong, silent man that he had always been.

And that was the thing; that was the deciding factor. Her father had actually asked for her help. He had come to her (no matter how he set it up and no matter the secrecy and the fights) and asked for her help. That's what it came down to. How could she say no?

'Father?' He looked up, and she looked him in the eye. 'I'll go,' she said.

'Are you sure? You can't go back on this decision.'

'Yes. I'll go.'

His shoulders relaxed and he smiled.

'Sharon has already told you the cover story.'

'It's very cloak and dagger. I'm not sure what I'm going to tell everyone.'

He smiled. 'You'll think of something. You'll work it out. I know this is odd, but it is an undercover assignment. I have no idea what you'll turn up. Just report whatever you find back to Sharon.' The smile disappeared as he stood up. 'And don't breathe a word to anyone.'

Reporting to Sharon. And Mel had hoped that this would lead to more time with her father, more communication. But it wasn't to be. She was just another employee after all. Ah well.

'We'll talk later,' he said as he left the room.

Mel slumped onto her chair her brain spinning, but she wasn't given much time to contemplate her actions. As quickly as her father left, Sharon arrived and took his place at the back of the black desk.

'So you're going to Lillyford?'

'It seems that way.' Mel could hardly believe it herself. 'Sorry for making this difficult for you. If I had known last week ...'

'I understand, you weren't to know.'

Sharon handed her a folder.

'You'll find the contract and all other information in here. Including a memory stick with everything we can work out about the issues. I'd like the contract signed and on my desk at the end of the day, if you can. Mr Thompson wants you out there as soon as possible.'

'Of course. I'll do that.'

'And Mel, if you could somehow make this stick with the other staff? I'll keep the story going once you've left but even I don't find this overly believable …'

Mel nodded but her stomach sank. This might be the hardest part of the whole job. How was she going to make this believable? She had been so strong about making her own way in the business. About doing it her way, by herself. How would she convince people that this was a sensible move?

Once again, Mel grabbed Evie on her way through the office. If anyone could help, Evie could. They'd been friends since high school, since Mel turned up at the boarding school lost and alone. Up until that time, Mel had been brought up by a string of *au pairs*—her mother had died at her birth and Mel felt that her father had spent more of his time building his business than investing in his own daughter. Apart from the distant father, Evie was one of the most constant influences in Mel's life. They had been through so many adventures together. Evie was the only one in the office who knew who Mel really was. And the only one in the office Mel truly trusted; and who was not a part of whatever this 'anomaly' was.

Once again, sitting over a mocha and a flat white, a slightly mollified Mel told her news.

'So, yes, I'm going to Lillyford now. And here's the thing, and I really need your help with this one—I need a believable story to tell the office. It's all very hush hush. I'm assuming you're not the mole, the bad guy doing whatever the bad guy is doing. But I'm not supposed to tell anyone at all. But everyone knows that I told them "no". And now I need to backflip. For no reason.'

'Oh, that's easy.' Evie waved her hand at Mel like she was brushing away a fly.

'Easy?' Mel sat up. 'This is the hardest part of the whole thing.'

'Nah, I'm just gonna say that they told you that you'll definitely miss out on the promotion to level four if you don't do this. That you'll have to wait another five years or whatever.'

'They won't believe I'd backflip over something like that.' Mel slumped back down into her seat and sipped her coffee.

'What, the level four promotion? The one you have worked towards, slaved over, talked about nothing else but, for this last six months? The one you're banking your next apartment on? The promotion you know you've got in the bag and no-one's going to take away from you? Mel, they'll believe it alright.'

'Have I really been that obvious?'

'Look, we all like a bit of ambition, but you're something else. It's like you're driven to get to the top. I don't know why, and it doesn't bother me, though I'll miss you when you're out of the office, whether it's to higher management or out in the boondocks. I sure won't be coming with you. I'm happy to stay right where I am.

'But if this was the thing standing in your way to an upward move I believe you'd do it. I'll just tell everyone that Sharon hadn't made that clear last week. That she told you this morning and you immediately flipped.

'And if people like Senka or Mandy don't believe that, then I'll tell them you heard this week about a really private, off-the-record spa resort there and that you're using the travel funds from the move to get you closer so you can just hang out at the spa and lounge around. It's something they would do so they'll probably fall for that.'

Mel pulled a face.

'Right, so now you're spreading two stories in the office that make me look really bad. Great. I'm so happy with that. Not!'

'Well I'm sorry. But it's all I have to work with.' Evie put on a fake pouty face. 'You ask me to do a hard job. I'm doing the best that I can. And it will work. Don't dis the methods of a true gossip artist.'

Mel leaned over the table and grabbed Evie's hand.

'I'm truly grateful. I really am. Just make sure you don't accidentally slip up and let out the real story of why I'm going.'

Evie smiled. 'I might *look* super blonde, but it's a disguise. Trust me, I'll look after you. I know what I'm doing.'

And that was that. Before she could really get her head around it, Mel's apartment was packed, the farewell lunch at the office was held, and she'd been given the nice gift of chocolate and bubbly and a card signed by everyone. Even Tom, though she was sure the words were meant with a touch of sarcasm. And she was on her way to whatever the country held.

Through the days of preparation she had carefully scanned her office-mates' faces, wondering if she could find out who was involved at the office before she left. But they all looked the same as they always had. Tom, just as slimy as usual; but Mel wasn't stupid enough to think that a personality clash meant an evil villain. Andrew, friendly, even charming at times, but was he charming his way through for his own purposes? Senka, stressed and harried, rushing from project to project, but was that because she was hiding a dreadful secret? And so on, and so on. Each of them could be a bad guy, each could just be a normal person trying to make it in a hard world. She had no training for this, no idea how she was going to meet her father's high expectations.

But she was going anyway. So that was that.

3

Mel sat in McDonalds nursing a strong, hot coffee. The chain store wasn't her first go-to for a top-up of her caffeine levels but today she didn't have any choice.

The last couple of weeks had been a whirlwind. Packing up the apartment, finding someone new to take over the lease, packing up her desk at work, training in the new techniques that she was going to teach the farmers. Mel's head was almost as full as her car.

All the big furniture and boxes were being brought by the removal company and would meet her at Lillyford tomorrow but somehow there was a whole heap of little bits and pieces that she had stuffed into her tiny yellow hatchback to bring over on the ferry with her. She was sure her belongings had multiplied as she'd packed them. Who knew you could fit so much stuff into a studio apartment?

Getting from Melbourne to Lillyford required either a plane trip or an overnight ferry ride and then a two-hour drive. The plane trip wasn't an option because Mel would need her car to get around all the farms. So the ferry it had to be. And it hadn't been the most pleasant of experiences.

Mel was sure it *could* be pleasant, but somehow she'd picked the day with the six-metre waves in Bass Strait. She had struggled to stay in her bunk in her little cabin and she was still going up and down now, even though she had been an hour or so on solid land. She wondered how long that would last.

And having to be up and off the boat at 5.30 a.m. was another strike against the whole system. They never promised to be a luxury cruise but surely they could change the timing just a little so that people could sleep until at least six. What kind of crazy people were happy to be up at 5 a.m.?

And that's why she was here at the 'little Scottish restaurant' as her father always called it. In Devonport there were no other cafés open at this stupid time of 6.30 a.m. There was nothing else open at all. It wasn't the most pleasant of welcomes. But at least she could get some caffeine into her system here.

Never had a McDonalds coffee tasted so good. Not that it was good as such, just necessary. She took her time over it. She didn't have to be at Lillyford until 2 p.m. or later for the bed-and-breakfast she was staying at for the first night. She could have a look around the countryside on her way. Maybe pull the car over at some place and have a nap.

She had the folder of information her father had given her safely stashed in her laptop bag in her car. She knew she should get her head around what little there was as soon as possible. She should have already looked at it so that she knew what she was getting herself into. But there had been no time, no time at all. And right now she didn't think she'd even be able to focus on the words.

No, the plan now was to get to Lillyford, and from there, to find the BnB and then maybe have a sneak peak at the house that would be her abode for the next little while.

She didn't even know how long she'd be staying in this town. As short a time as possible, if it had anything to do with her. Then she'd move back to somewhere with decent coffee early in the mornings.

To: Evie
Subject: Living in a Cavern

Dear Evie,

Well. I made it. Who knew that a studio apartment could hold so much stuff? Compared to a car, anyway.

My tiny little bright yellow hatchback was filled to the absolute brim. I had even wound down the back windows a bit, tucked stuff through them, and then wound them back up. Thank goodness for electric windows. Of course, I couldn't see anything through the rear window and that was a bit scary when the huge trucks were bearing down on me on the highway. I am now an expert in the use of side mirrors.

I arrived yesterday afternoon and stayed the night in a BnB. All my furniture (such as it is) will turn up sometime today. I'm writing this from my new house while I'm waiting for the truck. Thank goodness for hotspot.

The BnB was nice. Comfortable. Lots of pine lining the walls, a small table and chairs, a kitchen, little bathroom. All about the same size as my studio. It was originally the owners' garage but they've converted it. I could have stayed there for the duration of my job here. I would have been happy enough.

But no. Instead I've been given a huge house. Well, huge-ish compared to my studio. It has three bedrooms. What am I going to do with three bedrooms? There will be plenty of space when you come over to visit.

The kitchen needs remodelling. The cupboards are all painted white, with those round metal door handles from the 70s or maybe even the sixties. There is one small section of drawers. That's it. The rest are 60s, some so high there's no way I can reach them. But I don't have enough stuff to fill them with so I guess they'll just stay empty. Or fill up with spiders and mice or whatever happens in the country.

The lounge room is across the hallway from the kitchen. No open plan stuff here. White lace curtains to stop the neighbours being nosy. My futon couch will be it for the lounge furniture. I think I'll set up my desk in the lounge room too so I can watch Netflix on my computer screen.

I'm going to rattle around in the house like a marble in a tin. Don't think cosy cabin, think massive cavern holding one person. I'll get my steps up walking from the kitchen to the nice green-walled bathroom with the big pink bathtub and pink sink. Can you hear the sarcasm screaming at you through your computer? This place sucks.

I hear a truck pull up to offload my meagre furnishings. I would drop down to Ikea to get more stuff to make this place homey but the nearest Ikea is a plane trip away.

Yours from her place of banishment,
Mel

To: Mel
Subject: Missing you

Oh Mellie, you poor thing. Sounds totally rotten. I don't know what I'd do in a place like that. You'll have to take up painting or something—cover the boring kitchen cupboards with artwork. If I had a niece or nephew I'd get them started on it for you. But sadly, my brother being such a slack bum, I cannot help.

It's been mad here already without you. I don't think anyone (apart from myself of course) really understood all the work you did. Tom is just not keeping up, and muggins here has been given the job of helping him out. The great temptation is, of course, to stuff him up so that management realises the huge mistake they've made and begs you to come back again. Though I guess your extreme competence is one of the reasons they have sent you over there.

I tried that new café for lunch today. You know the one just down on the corner? Replaced the terrible sushi place. They make this thing called a mega-bowl. It was amazing—brown rice as a base (I left most of that, carbs you know) and then avocado, beets, bean sprouts, a bit of chicken, lentils, just gorgeous. I know where I'll be going whenever I'm feeling like being healthy. Though I don't think having me as a customer twice a month is going to help them survive :-)

Must run—financials are due on Friday and I've tried and tried to get Senka to send me their stuff by email but I'm going to have to ring her and that will be another hour wasted. I can do without this.

Enjoy your holiday getting settled.

Yours from the rat race,

Evie

To: Evie
Subject: What holiday?

What holiday Evie? Where is the beach? The sunshine? The margaritas by the pool?

I'll tell you something. It's super creepy here at night. SUPER creepy.

I mean, I live in an apartment. I'm used to night noises. Heck, I'm used to the crazy homeless woman who just goes up and down my street screaming at night for no reason. You remember her, don't you? But this place? It's so quiet, and then I swear when I was in bed last night I could hear someone walking around. Walking around in my house. And there's no one here to be doing the walking.

I don't believe in ghosts. If I did, I would have been down at the BnB place knocking on their door asking them to let me stay there. I don't know what it was. But it was super creepy, I'm telling you.

And then at 4 a.m. or something, the rooster next door started crowing and all the birds started singing. And that was the end of my extremely non-restful sleep for the night.

This is not a holiday. Far from it.

Thanks for your ideas re decoration. I'm not going to worry about it too much. I keep telling myself that I'm only here for the short term. I just need to figure out what's going on here and make it stop. Then I can head back to Melbourne and Tom can come out here and finish off the environmental change stuff and we can have our nice cosy office back just the way we like it.

I just need to put up with things for a little while. No point in going to any great effort to make it too comfortable.

I don't want to get more furniture, that's for sure, that would just be a waste. There's no way I'm going to have a place this size when I get back to the city!

Tell me everything that's going on back there. I am missing our cosy chats!

See you soon, I hope, if I survive this experience,
Mel

4

Mel *was* bored. Leaving Melbourne had been such a panic. There was so much to do and she wasn't sure she'd get it all done. She'd been working sun-up to sun-down and then packing through to midnight. She'd redirected mail, paid bills, found someone to take over her lease, and cleaned until her arms ached. And at work she'd completed reports, made sure files were labelled properly, sorted out everything for handover and then packed again. Every second of her life had been scheduled for one (or more) jobs. She'd barely had time to eat. Exercise had gone out the window for the last two weeks. It had been crazy.

And then she'd got on to the ferry and from that moment life had been empty. She'd been given a few days to settle in before starting work. The days stretched out in front of her. There was nothing to do. She knew no-one. She didn't even have the internet at her new house yet.

She felt a bit bad for complaining to Evie about the house. Mel was the one who had chosen it, after all. She had looked at a website for five minutes and then chosen this place because it was close to the centre of town. There wasn't a lot of choice. But she couldn't even recall looking at the photographs of the internal rooms. It was quite a shock to see the pink bathtub and sink in the bathroom. But there had been so much to do.

Maybe she should have waited until she got here, spent a couple more nights in the BnB and figured out what she actually wanted. But then, there were no houses smaller than this. Not really. And she sure as hell didn't want to be living in a house with other people. Sharing a bathroom? No thanks. And the BnB would have been too expensive to stay in for the months that she would be here. So this was the place she had.

She unpacked her boxes, putting one of the bedrooms to good use for storing empties. She took her time figuring out where she wanted things to go. She cleaned too. Scrubbed every cupboard out. Vacuumed all the carpet. Music on in the background. But what she had written to Evie was true. The lounge room looked empty with a single couch and a desk and computer. The dining-table-for-one fitted into the kitchen, and the dining room was not needed. The second and third bedrooms were completely empty if you didn't count the empty boxes. Mel didn't even bother folding the boxes away. They just sat in the bedroom ready to receive her goods as soon as she could pack up again and get out of there.

She knew she needed to get out and get to know Lillyford. For one thing, the groceries she'd brought with her were nearly gone, and she couldn't stay in the house forever. She knew that the feverish unpacking and cleaning had just been a way to keep busy and a way to stop herself from facing the town that she would have to call home for the next few months. But she really didn't want to. As long as she was in this house she could pretend that it was just a holiday or just an aberration, a blip on her lifeline.

She looked in the fridge again and decided she had enough for one more night. She would get groceries tomorrow. Tomorrow she would leave the house. But tonight she was tired from the unpacking and cleaning, and from the early mornings and restless nights.

She massaged her stiff shoulders and decided she would give the pink bath a go. She would see just what it was like. She was sure she couldn't get a decent massage in this place, but maybe if the bath was deep enough she wouldn't need to.

Maybe she could get used to this, she thought as she lowered herself into the steaming water. Maybe the whole thing would feel like a holiday.

Five minutes later she realised just how bored she was. She hadn't spent this much time with her own thoughts for … well probably since she was locked in her own room after lights out in the hostel in high school. It wasn't that pleasant, the time spent with her own thoughts. Her thoughts were repetitive and negative, worrying about whether she was going to make it, whether she was going to get anywhere in life. Worrying about whether she would end up old and alone. She was going to have to find something to do to keep herself occupied.

It was time to look at the folder from her father.

Dressed in a comfortable dressing gown and with her hair wrapped in a towel, Mel settled back on the futon and opened the folder. It was quite a skinny folder, not a whole lot of information, but there was the usb key as well. What was it that had got her father so concerned that he had sent her on this wild goose chase?

Maybe she would look it over and find nothing and realise that it was her father just trying to build her character or something again. But she hoped not.

But as she looked, she became intrigued, almost against her will. It was hard to narrow it down further than the Lillyford region but there were more issues coming out of this place than there should have been. Definitely more than the regular count of issues.

Weights that varied just a little bit, delivery times that varied by just a few days. And here, a truck where the refrigeration failed but the mechanics couldn't figure out why, and here another one just a month or so later. And then, and she remembered this one, the container that went missing and turned up a week later. She remembered Tom working hard on figuring out what happened but not being able to make head nor tail of it. The driver—did he talk to the driver? She couldn't quite remember now and the records were incredibly unclear.

Almost like someone was deliberately messing it up. Fudging it a bit.

But why? What possible good could come from making the region look unreliable? Was it a case of sabotage?

Did the problems stem back to any one farm? They didn't seem to. If anything, Hopwoods was mentioned more than anything else, and maybe Northfield, but the issues were spread over all the farms in the area. And of course, these things were normal, so some of the issues could be just regular issues. It was just that the frequency was much greater than normal.

That would be one of her jobs, ferreting out the normal from the abnormal. But really, something was definitely going on. Or if it wasn't, someone needed to take these farms in hand and get them to up their game. And it looked like Mel was that someone.

She'd better put on her superhero cape and get on with the job then.

5

To: Mel
Subject: There's nothing happening here

Oh dear, that sounds awful. I agree, the sound of traffic rumbling by, and even your normal sounds of people in the apartments around you and stuff, I can't imagine how it would be without that. Super creepy.
Tom says he reckons the noise of someone walking in your house is probably just the house cooling down. He used to live in a house that did that. Not out in the country, of course.
We went to the rooftop bar last night just to hang out, and they were showing a movie. It was so much fun, all of us sitting in beanbags on the roof watching this crackup of an independent film. All slapstick. We missed you. Truly. You would have loved it.
Senka was a bit of a worry. She sat morosely in a corner and drank far too much and then when it started to kick in she was honestly a bit manic. When I left she was draped over some guy's shoulders singing at the top of her lungs. I didn't think to ask whether she had driven herself there. I mean, she was hilarious, but there are limits, aren't there? I hear tell she's been rapped over the knuckles by Sharon a couple of times too. It makes you wonder what's going on.
Otherwise, life is the same in this miserable place. There's not much to tell. Someone has been stealing food from the fridge—Nigel had his half-eaten noodle box go missing. He's threatening to add laxatives to it if it happens again. Maybe it's Senka. It doesn't bother me of course, I don't have time to eat lunch most days, as you know, I just duck down to get a latte and then it's back on with it. Somehow it doesn't make any difference to my waistline though. You'd think that fasting lunch would help me be more svelte.
See you soon, I really hope you're right about this being a short-term thing,
Evie

Mel sighed. If that email was supposed to make her feel better, Evie didn't know how to do it. Nothing happening, just a rooftop cinema experience. Even the story of someone stealing food from the fridge was at least something. And poor Senka, you'd think someone would talk to her, find out what really was going on, not just make up stories behind her back. And Tom was sticking his nose into the emails she sent to Evie? That was nearly enough to make her pack up and head back, just to slap some sense into Evie. What was that girl doing showing her emails to Tom?

Mel was going to write back immediately but then she looked out the window. The sky was a clear blue, bright blue, white fluffy clouds. It was a gorgeous day outside. Not a smudge of pollution anywhere. Suddenly she needed to be out of the house. She'd spent far too long in those four walls. The suburban three-bedroom house was bigger than her Melbourne studio apartment, sure, but there was a wide world out there to explore and she decided to go explore it.

She pulled on her active wear and tied her hair in a ponytail. This felt more like it. More normal. She took one step out the door and breathed deeply. The air smelled heavenly. The birdsong was beautiful. Her spirits lifted. This was what she needed—a jog. She should have known she was missing it. She jogged every day at home.

She didn't need any cars or traffic lights getting in her way so she decided to take one of the roads leading out of the town. Once she'd jogged for a while she was sure her head would feel clearer and she would be able to face anything.

One foot after the other, that's what it was about. Earbuds in, music loud. Pure joy.

That was until the log truck drove up behind her, blaring its horn. Mel screamed and flung herself into the hedge on the side of the road. She hadn't heard the truck coming until it was right on top of her. There were no footpaths, there was nowhere to go. This road might have been a highway but it was very narrow, especially when you put a log truck onto it.

Pulling twigs out of her hair, Mel tried to slow her breathing and pull herself together. The road that had been a place of freedom just thirty seconds before, was now a terrifying house of horrors.

How many more trucks would be rolling through? Mel didn't want to take her chances. She pulled out her earbuds and ran straight back into town.

Once she got to the safety of more suburban roads, still no footpaths but small enough that there were unlikely to be trucks either, she felt safer. The cars would be going slower here. They'd see her. She could jog around the block a bit. See a bit of the town. It wasn't quite the freedom of the open road, but it was still outside.

It was interesting too. Beautiful old weatherboard houses, painted white and yellow and blue, with large verandas out the front. Some were even older, well probably older, they were brick houses, two storey, tiny windows, high peaked roofs with lacey gables. Utterly delightful but probably cold and draughty to live in.

And so many beautiful gardens. There were bulbs everywhere, bright yellow daffodils—Mel could recognise those—but also blue and white and multicoloured bulbs and other flowers she couldn't name at all. Big bushy plants all covered in flowers at the front door of one place, and another garden with little rock beds everywhere and flowers peeking out of gumboots and watering cans. How lovely to be here in the spring!

Some of the trees were showing new growth, tiny bright green leaves covering all the branches. Some were still completely bare. And the hills were the olive green of the Australian gum.

Lulled into a sense of security, she began once more to enjoy the jog. One foot in front of the other. She was about to put her earbuds back in when she passed by a blue weatherboard house with a white picket fence. And a big black dog sitting on the front veranda.

The dog rushed at the fence barking and growling. Mel's leisurely jog turned into a flat out sprint. She didn't stop until she got home, which was, fortunately, just around the corner. She didn't look back to see whether the dog was following her, looking back would have slowed her down. Her hands shook wildly as she tried to fit her key into the front door lock. She didn't feel safe again until the door was firmly closed behind her and she was leaning up against it.

She was never going to be able to jog here. Everything was out to attack her. Going across fields would be just as dangerous, probably snakes or drop-bears out to get her.

She took a shower and calmed down a little. Cup of coffee in hand, she decided to write back to Evie and then watch some online television. She had been trying not to do too much of that; her phone was providing all her internet and she knew the data bill could get immense very quickly. But right now she needed a lot of distraction and calming and she had no idea how she was going to lever herself out of the house again. Today's attempt had been a roaring failure.

Oh well, at least she had some news to tell Evie, at least something had happened today.

To: Evie
Subject: It gets worse

Dear Evie,
I'm going to tell you my latest adventure, but first:
YOU SHOWED MY EMAIL TO SLIMY TOM?
What the hell? Who cares what he thinks the noises in my house are?
Who cares what he thinks at all?
And what if I had told you something confidential?
Anyway, back to the adventure: Today I decided I'd been slack for too long and that I needed to go for a jog. It was probably your comments about being svelte. Do you think that your regular 3 p.m. chocolate from the donations box might have something to do with your waistline? Keep going to that healthy place. They probably do takeaway and you could eat at your desk.
And don't mention lattes to me either. I miss good coffee. I'm so happy that I have my bench top machine but the coffee is not the same from those little pods. It's just not good enough. I haven't been game to try anything in town. I've just been pottering around my house and eating the food I brought with me. But I'll have to bite the bullet soon. Find a supermarket, or go the hour-long drive to a proper town.
Anyway, the adventure. Here it is: I went for a jog. You might think that there is nothing new about that. I mean I always jog, every day. But this was definitely a new thing.
To set the scene, there are no footpaths here. None outside my house anyway. I saw footpaths on the Main Street when I drove in, but as you go out from there they disappear very quickly. And I didn't want to make a spectacle of myself jogging, it's not how I want to make my first impression on the locals. So I headed away from town out along my street. Well, pretty quickly I had to turn on to the highway. Not that it's a freeway or anything. Just one lane each way. And no footpath on the side.
I was enjoying the jog. The air here is delicious, there's no gainsaying it. It's just sweet to smell. There's no pollution. The water is amazing to drink too—no chemical taste at all, just like the best bottled stuff, straight out of the tap.
So as I was saying, the air smelled sweet until I went past a cow paddock, then I nearly had to stop and upchuck on the side of the road. How do people work with cows? But I kept going and got past that OK and was having a nice think to myself, music going in my ears. My brain

33

was really clearing for the first time since I got here, and I was thinking that it wouldn't be too bad.

And then a truck nearly ran right over me. A massive semitrailer loaded with tree trunks bore down on me, horn blaring. There was nowhere to go. No footpaths. I had to jump off the side of the road into a hedge of some sort. Freaked me right out.

After the truck passed I brushed myself off, then turned around straight away and headed back to home. I thought that if I couldn't run along the highway, at least I could run down the streets of the town. There wouldn't be huge semis there throwing me into the bushes at the side of the road. But I was wrong.

I'm jogging along a nice suburban-looking street. The blocks are really big, the houses set right back from the road, but just tiny little fences. And that's important, the size of the fences, because I just about jumped out of my skin when a huge black dog started barking his head off at me as I went past his place. I freaked out, I think I screamed, and doubled my speed. I don't know if he was chasing me, he could easily have made it over the fence.

So that's it. That's probably the end for my skinny body. Or I'll have to buy a treadmill. I can't run here. I'll die. I'll be hit by a truck, or torn apart by rabid dogs, or killed by some tramp and buried in a shallow grave in the bush a few metres off the road, never to be seen or heard from again.

I'd like to sit in safety all day but I'm going to brave the Main Street (the opposite direction from the dog) and see what the little grocery shop here is like. I need more food, I'm running out.

Wish me luck, and if you don't hear from me in a day or so, notify the police.

Yours, scared stiff,
Mel

To: Mel
Subject: You crack me up

Dear Mel,
If you don't want Tom hearing your news then you shouldn't send me
emails that send me into fits of laughter at the desk. I crack up, I was
nearly crying from your last story, and of course, he asks what's going
on. He's sitting at your desk after all. Sitting so close it's a bit hard to hide
what you're doing from each other.
BTW he tells me that the dog was just defending its house from you and
it would never jump the fence. That's apparently just what dogs do.
We have to make our presentations at the end of the week. I still haven't
heard from Senka. I'm beginning to stress about it. Like I can put the rest
of the stuff into the powerpoint but I don't know what's holding her up.
How hard can it be? Maybe she should have been sent to outer woop-
woop instead of you. Maybe she's having a nervous breakdown. I just
don't know. We might send her to you for a health cure. Although with
your luck I'm not sure that would be a safe thing to do.
I guess you'll meet the farmers soon. Tell me if there are any cute ones.
Striding around the countryside with their shirts off. Oooo I can just
imagine it now.
I wish I had more news to tell you, but it's just same old same old here.
Too much to do, not enough time to do it in, I can see Tom and me
staying late tonight to get the stuff from Senka into order, if she finally
sends it.
Chocolate at 3 p.m. is a necessity, not a luxury, and I'd like you to
remember that.
It will probably be chocolate at 7 p.m. and again at 9 p.m. tonight. I'd die
without that donations box.
Keep telling me everything, your stories are so great,
Evie

'Keep telling me everything'. Mel realised that was something she couldn't do. She had been hoping to have Evie as her connection to the office but she realised now that she had no way of knowing if the mole or the bad guy was going to see her emails or not. So apart from the occasional phone call it was safer to keep it all to herself. And just report to Sharon like she'd been told to do.

She hoped there wouldn't be any more 'hilarious' stories coming from when she started the job-proper tomorrow. What else could possibly go wrong? And how was it already going wrong when she hadn't really started yet?

This whole thing was a huge mistake. She wanted to write to her father and tell him so. Tell him to send someone else.

But no. She had to think sensibly.

She hadn't really given it a go yet. And when she thought back to the contents of the folder, well, she was curious. Her interest was piqued. She would stay.

But hopefully she would also stay out of the way of massive scary dogs and murderous trucks.

As she drifted off to sleep, listening to the creaks and groans of the house that were slowly becoming familiar, she wondered what the morning would bring.

6

Mel squeezed herself into a pencil skirt and put on some heels. Lying around the house in her yoga pants had been just too comfortable and getting dressed for work felt like an imposition. She was sure she'd regret the shoes too—today was a day for moving into the office and setting it up. But today was also a day for first impressions. She'd weighed things up and decided skirt and heels was the way to go.

She'd stored the boxes for the office in the back of her hatchback, and she had her laptop and stand and keyboard sitting on the passenger seat in the front. She wondered what sort of setup would be waiting for her. All that she had been given was an address and she'd been told that her office would be in a shared building in the centre of town.

It didn't take long, just two minutes really, to get to the centre of town. Past a supermarket she'd have to visit as soon as possible and past the pub and a comfortable-looking café. They both looked OK from the outside but she wasn't sure she was ready yet to give them a go. She was suspicious that the café would sell instant coffee, and that the pub would deep fry everything and sell Vic Bitter and XXXX, and probably a house red and a house white. She just couldn't face it. She knew she'd have to soon; she was getting so bored and she needed to get to know some new people. But one thing at a time.

Today's thing was the office.

The address led her to one of the few two-storey buildings in the town. She parked directly in front of the building and tried to take it in. It was an old place, built in the early part of last century. A gracious old building with the look somewhat spoiled (in Mel's eyes) by the craft shop that was taking up most of the ground floor. Quilts and hand-made dolls, knitted jumpers and scarfs, cards and artwork and hanging macramé pot plant holders spilled out of every where. The look was cosy but cluttered. Not what you'd call refined. And Mel would have to walk through that to get to the stairs to go up to her office each day.

Well, today was the day she'd have to start. She walked around to the back of her car and pulled out a box. Suddenly a lady materialised next to her. Mel had never seen anything like her before. She had long grey curly hair, she looked about sixty, she was wearing a green dress with red floral patches on it. And a long hand-knitted olive green cardigan, and a knitted hair band, and she was wearing Crocs and socks on her feet.

Mel just blinked and stared. She had no words. It was obvious that this woman didn't care about fashion as such. She liked colour and she was going to go with it.

'Good morning!' said the apparition cheerfully.

'Uh, morning,' said Mel much less cheerily. It was hard to talk when you were trying to scrape your chin off the ground.

'I'm Merryn. I run Crafty Kitten here.' Merryn waved her hands in the direction of the dolls and piles of wool. 'I take it you're Mel? Coming to join us in the building?'

'Yes, that's me. How did you know?'

'Oh love, I know everything that's going on here. You'll get used to it. Can I help you carry anything in?'

'Um, if you want to. I …'

But Merryn had already reached into the boot of the car and grabbed one of the heavier boxes. She seemed to have no trouble picking it up and Mel hitched up her own box and trailed along in her wake as she strode into the building with a 'Don't worry about locking up dear, it will all be safe here,' floating on the breeze behind her.

They made their way through the hanging macramé pot plant holders and the piles of quilting fabric and through the back door of the shop. A set of steep and narrow stairs rose on the right of the narrow, windowless hallway. Merryn headed up the stairs and Mel followed to find another narrow hallway with a window at the end and a couple of doors opening off the sides.

'Here's your office, dear,' said Merryn opening a door. She put her box on the desk and Mel followed suit and then stepped back to have a look around. Her new office was a small but well-proportioned room. One wall was covered with inbuilt book shelves, and the desk and filing cabinet were against the opposite wall. On the outer wall of the building was a wooden sash window and Mel looked forward to seeing what the view was like, but she didn't have time right now. Merryn had already moved out of the room and was calling her.

'You'll find the communal kitchen down the hall here. There's a kettle and a fridge. We try to keep it all shipshape and fresh here. We don't employ a cleaner or anything and I'll be telling you if you need to do something to clean up.'

Mel followed the voice in a bit of a daze.

'And, you'll get to know the rest of us here as well. We have Henry and Jo, they are the hearing technicians. They work up here, though come to think of it they should be working downstairs. We might have to find a way to work that out. None of the oldies here should be made to walk up and down those narrow stairs. I'll have to see if I can change that. And you might see Mr Trevayne occasionally. He has the other room up here. He's a writer but he's not doing all that much writing right now if you ask me. He needs to either get on with it or give his office to someone else. But there's no talking to him. He's always run his own way, has Clancy. Does his own thing.

'Emma, now she works across the street in the information centre, but she comes in here quite often before and after her shifts. Likes to hang out in my shop for a bit of company. She's a lovely girl, but she needs to be more ambitious. Maybe you could show her how to get out and make something of herself? A city girl like yourself, I'm sure you could do her some good. I'll get her to come up and say hello. So there you go, love. Happy? Let's get some more of those boxes …'

Mel hadn't said a word but apparently Merryn didn't need her to, she could hold a conversation all by herself. And somehow, without listening, she knew exactly what was going on. Maybe she was a witch …

'You'll be here for a few months? Yes, I'm sure it's a bit of a shock to the system being in this sleepy place after living in Melbourne. But you'll get used to it. And don't let those farmers push you around. You'll know what they need, I'm sure of it.'

Up and down the stairs they went with a running commentary all the way. Mel wondered if she'd be able to get away and get any work done. She would have to be rude and tell Merryn to go eventually. She wasn't here to entertain, she was here to work. But when the little car was empty again Merryn melted away back into her shop and Mel was left in the office to unpack.

She breathed out, left the boxes to look after themselves for a minute, kicked off her shoes, and headed to the window to see what her view was like. Would it just be houses and rooftops? But no, she looked out over the river. The river the ford was named after, she guessed. It was beautiful, quite large, running freely.

There were a few native trees along the river but most were deciduous and had only the first blush of green—more a promise than the presence of new leaves. It would be absolutely gorgeous when they were all green, Mel thought, and then autumn with the reds and golds. Well, she wasn't going to be here to see it was she? She'd be long gone by then. But it would be a shame. Maybe she'd come back to visit, just to see.

And there, through the branches she could see a playground, an old fashioned one with an actual train that kids could climb all over, and seesaws and swings. And wonder of wonders, a path along the side of the river. A footpath that stretched as far as Mel could see. And people walking and jogging on it.

She wanted to head home, put on her joggers and go for a jog immediately but she was at work now. She had to get started. Reluctantly, she pulled herself away from the view and started to unpack boxes and set up her computer.

She sat down at the computer to write to Evie and realised that she hadn't linked in to the internet. She was hoping there was wireless available here as part of the package. The office had said something about it. She needed to find that email. She needed to stop using her own phone for internet, especially for work internet. She couldn't afford to keep going like she had been.

A tentative knock on the door stopped her furious searching through her inbox. She looked up. It obviously wasn't Merryn, she would have barged in and Mel would have heard her already. She would have been talking from halfway up the stairs. Instead a red-headed, freckle-faced girl of about twenty leaned in through the doorframe.

'Hello?' said Mel.

'Hi, I'm Emma,' said the face.

'Pleased to meet you.' Mel stood and shook hands.

'Merryn thought you might like me to get you a coffee?'

'Sure.' Mel expected Emma to head to the kitchen but instead she turned and went downstairs. And Mel grabbed her purse and phone and followed. She felt like she was going to spend all of today following. But whatever Merryn said about the place being safe, she was going to take her valuables and close her door.

Emma led the way over the road back up the hill a bit to the café Mel had seen earlier. Mel could smell the rich aroma of coffee as she followed, and the smell of freshly baked bread too. It was heavenly.

So it looked like she was wrong about the country café. The name, Mummy's, didn't promise much, or maybe it was just that Mel had never experienced a mother's cooking. But the scents wafting out promised so much more.

Mummy's had outdoor seating surrounded by lavender and roses, a veranda, and some indoor seats.

'Want to sit out here?' Emma asked.

Mel shivered, 'It's a bit cool.' Did it ever get really warm in Tasmania? What good was outdoor seating in this place?

Emma led the way indoors and they took a table by the window.

'I hope you'll like the coffee,' said Emma.

'It smells heavenly.'

'Oh yes, these guys roast their own. We're very into good coffee here.'

A tattooed waitress in a white shirt and black skirt and apron came to take their order. Mel ordered her usual flat white and Emma, after hearing the order, decided to have the same.

'I normally have a cappuccino,' she said sheepishly. 'I like the chocolate.'

'Lots of people do,' said Mel, 'my workmate always has a mocha.'

'What's that?'

'Even more chocolate. Half chocolate, half coffee,' Mel smiled. This girl was such a baby, she had no idea.

With her first sip of coffee Mel relaxed. She was so happy to be wrong about the coffee and she wondered what else she'd be wrong about. She had been making judgements of the country town without any basis in fact.

Although there had been things that she hadn't even thought about that she wished she'd had some facts on. Like cow pats, and barking dogs, and creaking houses. She wasn't a country girl just yet.

She realised she'd been silent now for about five minutes, just enjoying her coffee. She was so used to being by herself she'd forgotten how to make conversation.

'So Emma, do you like living here?' The question was supposed to be small talk but Emma gulped and nervously pushed her hair back from her face.

'I guess so, I've never lived anywhere else.'

'What do you want to do with your life?'

'I just ... I don't know. I'm pretty happy working in the info centre. You know, short shifts, ten to two, plenty of time to do other stuff around the place.'

'That sounds like there's a "but" there ...'

'Well ... I'd love to be a vet. But I can't.' Emma looked down at her coffee.

'Why not?'

'Oh, you can't train for that here. You have to go to the mainland and do uni and ... I dunno.'

Mel smiled a little at that term 'the mainland'—that's what these people living on this island called the main continent, was it? Interesting.

'But you've finished school, right? Got the marks to go do it?'

'Oh yeah, I did really well at school. But I'm just not sure if I can move all the way over there.' Emma gave a nervous giggle. 'And then I got the job here, helping out tourists and all, and it's ... it's fine.'

'I guess it's good to have a job.'

'And I'm not picking veggies or whatever. It's a good job. And I feel useful.'

'Well, sure.' Mel could see what Merryn was saying about Emma not being ambitious. But she didn't see that it was her job to force a girl to go to all that risk just to be a vet. The thought of doing that job made

Mel shudder. She wouldn't want to be operating on sick animals. She just couldn't see the joy in it anywhere.

She drained her cup, enjoying it to the very last sip.

'I'd better get back to it. Emma, do you know if I can get internet access over there?' She waved at their building over the road.

'Oh sure. Didn't Merryn give you the password?'

'No.'

'She's funny.' There was that giggle again. 'She just forgets that we'll need it for everything. I have to help her with her accounting every month or so, she just forgets what she needs to do online, or clicks the wrong thing. But that's OK. But that's another thing. If I go away to university, who will help Merryn out?'

'I'm sure someone would step up.'

'Well, anyway. It's not something I have to think of right now. Come on over with me and I'll get you set up.'

Mel paid for both coffees despite Emma's protestations and they headed back. This was not going to be anything like the office in the city, but Mel thought she could make it work.

To: Evie
Subject: First day

Dear Evie,

After much discussion with Merryn who runs the craft place downstairs, and Emma, a tiny slip of a red headed girl of about 20 who mans the info centre across the road, I have internet access. NBN even. At least here in my office. I won't have it at home for a while. Emma reckons that it will take months for them to hook me up. I'm not sure it's even worth trying. I don't suppose you could read this in your lunch hour? Somewhere where Tom can't hear your screams of laughter? Or that you could stop laughing at my utter misfortune? I didn't ask for this you know.

(And speaking of the slimy Tom, how does he know anything about the dog that was barking at me? He wasn't here. I tell you, it was a huge dog. The three-headed dog from Harry Potter had nothing on its drooling jaws and horrible growling bark. I just about leapt out of my skin.)

Anyway, I'm here and nearly set up in my new office.

I'm in a two-story building in the middle of the town. Red brick with sandstone surrounds for the windows and some sort of lace stuff (I think it's wood, not steel lace) on the really steeply pitched roof. It's old. There are even some fireplaces—all closed in and not used now but the chimneys reach out of the roof. It's a large building for this place. Sounds weird to say that after working on the 16th floor, but I'm already acclimatising to everything being just one level and in this tiny town there are only a few places that go up two floors, one of them being this place, and another, the pub.

My office is up the stairs and towards the back. There's a little window that looks down on the river (more about that later, I made a brilliant discovery). It's a tiny little office. I reckon I have about as much space in the office as I had in the cubicle I shared with you. Enough for a desk and a filing cabinet. Not much more than that.

It doesn't matter that it's so tiny though. I won't be having meetings here. The farmers won't be coming in to town, I have to go to them. So I'm going to be doing a fair bit of driving. Ah well, petrol is all provided. And I don't mind driving, as long as I don't run across too many of those huge trucks. (I was going to say "run into" but I guess I shouldn't run into trucks at all.)

So I won't be spending too much time in this tiny room. The visits start tomorrow. Sharon wasn't wrong—we're getting produce from heaps of farms in this area. Crazy.

You'll want to know about the other people who share the building with me. Well, there's a craft place on the ground floor. That's the front room on the right. Merryn (who owns the place) makes all kinds of stuff, hats, quilts, scented candles. Anything craft, she makes it. She sells her stuff in one room and then she sells the raw ingredients, as it were, from the room on the other side of the front door. You know, wax, paint, wool, material, that sort of stuff. I think she makes all her own clothes. She is the most colourful person I have ever met in my whole life. It's like she doesn't care what she wears as long as it's colourful. I think one of my fun daily activities will be finding out what Merryn is wearing today. There's a sign in the window to say she runs a knitting class for beginners once a week. I'll be interested to see who turns up to that. And there are a couple more offices up here with me. One's a hearing centre—you know, where you can get your hearing aids. The other one apparently houses an author. Merryn says that he works there but she also said that he's, 'not writing enough lately'. She keeps tabs on everyone. I'm sure I'll hear about it if I don't get my work done. The hearing centre wasn't open today so I haven't met those people yet. Then, of course, there's Emma. She doesn't work in the building, her job is the info centre just across the road. But it doesn't feel like she's rushed off her feet in there and she spends a fair bit of her time over here with Merryn, before and after her shifts, and also when there are no tourists to chat with. Emma is about 20, she probably started doing the work straight out of high school. Born, raised, and trapped. She wants to be a vet but doesn't want to leave the state to have to study. I guess that's what happens.

To be thorough in my description, the final thing on my floor is the communal kitchen. So I'll be getting to know the other occupants as we meet over the water cooler (or over the kitchen tap, no water cooler here). Of course, there's no coffee machine in the kitchen. But the café over the road makes heavenly coffee. They roast their own. So that's one amazing discovery that's going to make life better.

And the other? There is a footpath next to the river. I saw it as I looked down on the river from my tiny window. I'm going to be able to run along the river! No trucks there. That should make my days go a lot more smoothly. I was really getting antsy at the thought of not being able to run.

Yours, in hope,
Mel

'Well, that day went well.' Mel exhaled as she slumped on to her futon couch and kicked off her heels. One day down, and goodness knows how many to go. She'd totally unpacked in the office, aware that she was sorting files into cabinets and arranging nicknacks on the bookshelf rather than getting her head into the things she was supposed to be doing.

But she was no detective. Where does one start to look for dodgy people? Especially when you're not sure what sort of dodgy you're looking for.

Maybe Merryn would know. Mel smiled at the thought. Wouldn't it be hilarious if Merryn was at the root of it all? The architect of some underworld drug-running business for which her craft shop and knitting group was just a front.

Nah, it wouldn't be her. She'd have bought some classier clothes if she was getting rich somehow.

But it would be worth chatting with Merryn to get the lowdown on the people in the town. She might let something slip that Mel could use to shed some light on the situation.

Anyway, tomorrow she would be spending time in the farms. She would be taking out the information that encouraged changes for more environmentally friendly farming. Even if she found nothing dodgy or illegal here, she could still make a change for good.

Educating farmers. That was just what she had planned to do with her life. Not.

She decided to spend a bit more of her phone data and watch something completely mindless on the internet before bed. Tomorrow was going to be another big day full of new things and she wasn't sure she was up to it.

7

Mel felt much more normal the next day. Her routine was back. She would get up and go for a jog, and then head in to work, buying a coffee on the way, and get started on the project of changing the world for the farmers.

She didn't worry too much about how she looked as she headed out for the jog. She wasn't going to see anyone that mattered. What really was important was that she could go down to the river and jog in peace without being afraid of trucks or dogs or any other scary thing this town had to offer.

She picked a route to the river that avoided the blue house with the picket fence. She savoured the morning air. The sky was filling up with grey clouds and it looked like the weather was going to turn later in the day, but for now it was a delicious morning. The birdsong was so beautiful that she even left her earbuds out for a while and just enjoyed the scenery and the sounds.

And that's how she heard the dog running up behind her. It was the same dog. The big black thing that had been barking at her before. She screamed and reached for the nearest thing she could find to protect herself. Which was a stick, about 30 cm long. Not a great weapon, but something.

'Get away from me,' she shouted, waving her stick in front of her.

The dog barked, and jumped at her. Mel screamed and jumped backwards to get away. She was looking wildly for a tree to climb when, calm as you like, the owner of the dog came jogging around the corner.

He took in the situation with one look and called, 'Bella. Sit.'

The dog barked again, but it sat down. It's eyes were focussed on the stick.

'Keep it away from me,' said Mel.

'What? Bella? She won't do you any harm. She thinks you're going to throw the stick for her. She loves to fetch a stick.'

Mel looked at the stick in her hand and hurriedly threw it to the side. The dog lunged after it and Mel screamed again.

The owner of the dog sighed, and clipped a leash on the dog's collar, and finally Mel relaxed enough to take her eyes off the dog and have a look at who this man was.

He was quite tall, fit and outdoorsy, with unruly blond hair, sunnies pushed to the top of his head, a black fleece jacket, and trackpants. He was standing now with hand outstretched to shake Mel's.

'I'm Jason, and this is Bella. I'm sorry she scared you. She really wouldn't hurt a fly, truly.'

'Uh, hi. I'm Mel.' Mel shook hands a little gingerly as doing so brought her closer to the dog. But now that she looked at the dog, sitting contentedly by her owner, tongue hanging out and tail wagging, she felt a bit of a fool.

'You're new here, right? Working for Thompson's?'

'Yes, I am. How did you know?'

'It's a small place.' Jason gave a shrug, then he gestured to Bella again. 'How about you give her a pat? Once she knows you she won't bark at you anymore. She just gets a little excited when it comes to strangers.'

'Um, no, I might pass at that,' said Mel. She really couldn't face it.

'Sure, no worries. Well then, Bella and I might keep jogging.'

'Right. Fine.' Mel returned Jason's wave and waited for them to get well ahead before she continued on her own. She also cut her jog short so that she could get back before Jason and Bella should follow her on the path. She might have known that the riverside path wasn't going to be any safer than anywhere else in this damned place. She would just have to get fat.

And she wished she hadn't been quite such an idiot in front of the guy. Because, to coin a phrase, he was quite dishy.

Cutting the jog short meant that she had plenty of time to shower and get changed into her work gear. She took the time too—today was the first day going out to the farms and she wanted to make a good impression. She was loaded with pamphlets and had slides on her laptop for a presentation. Everything was neatly stacked in her briefcase.

She put on a pencil skirt and a crisply ironed white blouse. She looked outside at the clouds roiling in the sky and added a cardigan to the outfit. Her suede heels completed the look and she was happy with herself as she headed to the café for the morning goodness.

She was very careful with the coffee, managing not to spill it down her front as she was sure she would do. These first days, they were the days when everything could go wrong. Coffee on your white shirt, ripping your skirt as you get out of the car, forgetting to put the important document in your briefcase, or forgetting to charge the laptop. She was determined not to make any mistakes. She had it all under control.

Mel found she was missing Evie's friendly face and sense of fun. She would have debriefed the whole dog incident with her if she'd still been in Melbourne and they would have laughed and commiserated together. Evie would have been so funny about the dishy bloke—Jason was his name, wasn't it?

It didn't really matter what his name was. Even if Mel saw him again she was sure there wouldn't be any friendly conversation. She'd made a fool of herself. And she didn't want to get to know that dog at all.

She was lost in her thoughts when a friendly voice called, 'Hi Mel.'

Mel looked up and saw Emma with a take-away coffee in her hand.

'Hi, how are you? Have a seat?'

Emma dithered a little but then sat. And Mel, desperate for some company, told her about the dog incident from the morning.

'Oh that's just Bella,' said Emma. 'She's a lovely dog once you get to know her. She's just a little playful still right now.'

Mel shivered expressively. 'If that was playful I'd hate to see her angry.'

Emma shrugged. Mel felt she was being given up as a lost cause.

'I'm just not sure what I'm going to do for exercise. There isn't a 24-hour gym here or anything is there?'

Emma laughed. 'No, no 24-hour gyms here. There isn't a gym at all, unless you count the weights that Angus has in his garage. I can't think of anyone who'd want to use one. But, well, you could …'

'What? I could what?'

'Well, I exercise my horse every morning. Would you like to come and join me? I'm sure I can find you something to ride.'

Mel cracked up, and tears smeared her mascara. She furiously dabbed at her eyes. Mel riding a horse? That was the best joke.

Eventually she pulled herself together.

'Thanks Emma but I might pass. I'll come and see you ride sometime though? Do you ride in a yard? Or out on the trail?'

'Oh both. But I'm training for dressage at the moment so I'm out there for a bit most mornings and then yeah, most Saturdays and Sundays. Whenever I can, you know?'

'What sort of horse do you have?'

'Oh Gypsy is only a thoroughbred.'

'Only? I thought that would be the best.'

'Not for dressage. A warmblood would be better. But I go with what I can afford, you know? She's beautiful though. So well behaved. We've worked so hard together.'

Mel drained the last of her coffee. She was grateful to Emma for listening, even though she was sure she didn't really understand Mel's fear. But she wasn't ready to hear someone wax lyrical about a horse. It was a whacking great animal, after all. Not a person. Though Emma seemed to think it was a person. She seemed to have a strong connection with the animal.

'I guess we'd better get on with our days.' Mel stood up.

Emma joined her. 'Oh yes, I should have been at work already. I guess it won't matter.'

'I hope I haven't got you in trouble.'

'It will be fine.'

Mel felt a lot less lonely as she crossed the road with Emma. Sometimes a friendly face is all you need.

As Mel packed her sunshiny car for the day and drove through the dirt roads to the farms she felt completely in control and happy. Even a few splatters of rain on the windscreen didn't break her mood. Today she was making her first steps towards getting this problem sorted, and getting back to the city. Shouldn't be too hard to see what was going on. And she could sort all these eco-problems at the same time.

She was good at presenting things, good at selling. She knew she could bring these farmers onside and get stuff done. Today was a day for being productive both in the surface job and the undercover one.

That feeling didn't last long.

It took a while to get to her first farm and the little car's juddering over the corrugations in the dirt road wiped a bit of the smile off her face. Her car wouldn't survive much of this kind of driving. She'd have to get the job done fast and get back to paved roads. But the dirt road went on and on, twisting around the side of the hills, and she started to wonder if she should turn back. She was about to pull over and check the map more thoroughly when she saw the sign at the gate for number 3117. Good. She was there.

The car shook again as she crossed the cattle grid then she drove past quite large paddocks, most of them green but one of them ploughed and showing the beautiful red earth full of the nutrients that gave this area such great vegetables. The driveway quality was worse than the road and Mel edged her car gingerly through a few potholes until she got to the buildings. There were a couple of large sheds, a house where the farmer obviously lived, and this little breeze-block building with a sign beside the door. Mel parked as close to that one as possible, thinking it was probably the right place. The rain was clearing to a light shower but she'd be happier inside, nevertheless.

She pasted her most professional look on her face, grabbed her briefcase, and stepped out of the car, straight into a mud puddle. The mud splashed right up the back of her leg and she looked in horror at her shoe. Mud splatters plastered the suede—gritty brown on the beautiful black.

She ran through the rain to the office and, once through the door, fished around in her briefcase to find something to wipe the mud off. The only thing she could come up with was a tiny tissue. She rubbed a bit but it was completely ineffective. Her smile was well and truly wiped off and she wasn't particularly polite as she introduced herself to the receptionist.

The receptionist told Mel that the grower ('the what?' said Mel, 'John Shackleton, the grower' the receptionist repeated more slowly, as if Mel was deaf) was out in the fields and pointed her in the general direction. 'He's checking on the crop this morning. He likes to get out there himself.'

There was no mention of him coming in anytime soon. No possibility that she would go out and get the farmer. And no invitation that Mel was welcome to wait indoors. The receptionist obviously expected her to go outside and meet Mr Shackleton there.

Mel looked at the rain, shuddered, then held her briefcase over her head and headed out to the field. Her heels sank into the ground and she felt goosebumps rising all over her arms and legs. She hadn't been this cold and uncomfortable since sports days in high school. Or this unsure of herself.

'Mr Shackleton?' she called, gingerly picking her way among the plants.

'That'd be me,' he replied, and stood and waited, arms crossed, for Mel to walk all the way out to where he was. John Shackleton was a man of about 60, with grey hair and a beard, his waterproof jacket stretched over his beer belly and fastened by one button at the front.

'Mr Shackleton, I'm Mel. I'm here to talk with you about the energy efficiency changes that Thompson's would like you to make. I'm sure you've seen some information in the post?' Mel opened her briefcase to pull out the flyers she had brought, but the farmer was not interested.

'Oh yes, those "save the planet" changes. You city greenies have no idea of how things work out here. Look, I'm not going to waste my time on that. Just let me do what I know how to do best and you stick with what you know.'

He turned his back on Mel and continued to inspect his plants.

'But ... uh ...' Mel stood rooted to the spot. She looked at her shiny pamphlets that were now being spattered with drops of rain and blown about in the wind, and then looked back at the farmer. This was not how it was supposed to go.

'You're not interested in looking after the planet?' she asked, dumbfounded.

'I'm interested in running my farm the way I know best. What do you know about farming?'

Mel tucked the pamphlets back into her briefcase and held the case back over her head to shield her from the rain. And she looked around the field, really seeing it for the first time.

Shackleton was right. She didn't even know what vegetables were being grown in this field. She had no idea about farming. And this man seemed to be one with nature—even the raindrops weren't bothering him. Of course, he was wearing warmer clothes, and a waterproof jacket. And he hadn't spent any time blowdrying his hair this morning either.

She must have looked pretty forlorn because Shackleton took pity on her. 'Look, if you come back here with some ideas of how this might benefit me, then I might be interested. But you can be sure I know what I'm doing here and I'm not going to take advice from someone who doesn't know a lettuce from a potato.'

Mel nodded, 'Right. I see your point. Well, I might come back to you later then.'

He nodded, 'You do that,' he said and turned back to checking the plants.

Mel picked her way back across the field, shivering as she went. This might be harder than she thought.

But once she was sitting in her car with the heater going and she began to warm up again, her natural optimism rose to the surface. Yes, she didn't know much about farming, but she'd done her homework on the environmental impact of the farms. She knew that if they changed their methods slightly, worked together to buy more efficient refrigeration, and simple things like better lightbulbs in the processing sheds, and then maybe even working on waste recycling to give better fertilisation processes, that they'd be able to save so much in greenhouse gasses and waste. It was the truth. It wasn't Thompson's primary focus of course, but it would be helpful to the farmers and helpful to the company as well. And though Shackleton looked one with the land, Mel cared about the planet too. She could have some input.

Maybe this guy was the exception. You could expect to meet grumpy old buggers out here in the country. There had to be some farmers who cared enough about the planet to want to help fix problems that were slowly killing it. She would try the next farm. It would go better. She had three on her list to visit today and this rejection would give her more time to work on the others.

Mel's little car shot along the highway towards the next farm, Northfield. She had a little difficulty finding it; she first took the wrong turn off the highway, the dirt road came to a dead end and a locked gate, and Mel had to make a scary three-point turn between two deadly ditches. She was grateful that the yellow hatchback was so small and manoeuvrable but she was also terrified that she'd get stuck in a ditch with no way to get herself out, and probably no mobile coverage if she needed to call for help.

After extricating herself from that situation she then found herself driving past the correct turnoff at 100 km/h with a ute up her tail so that she couldn't slow down to turn around. She made it eventually though, down a narrow dirt road which she would have driven on slowly whether there was anyone behind her or not. It was a good thing she was driving slowly because the signage on the correct driveway consisted of a white-painted square of board with a number written on it. The sign looked like it had been made thirty years ago and she could hardly read the number. Did people just expect people to know? Maybe this is why the trucks were getting lost or damaged. Maybe it was something as simple as bad signage and dreadful roads.

She picked her way slowly up the driveway, trying to dodge the worst of the potholes, and the branches reaching out from beside the road scratched along her windows.

It wasn't a long driveway. She ended up at a weatherboard farmhouse that needed a good coat of paint, with windowsills rotting off and the windows curtained by tattered rags. Next to the house was a small garden, it was filled with weeds, but even so Mel could see that it was used for smaller plantings of varied kinds. She guessed it was a kind of kitchen garden growing vegetables for the family. Not that anyone had spent time in it lately. It was pretty overgrown.

Her stomach sank and she clenched her fists so hard that her nails dug into her palms. She couldn't see how this farm would be any better than the last one. If they weren't willing to put money into maintenance, why would they put money into the environment?

But then, maybe if she focussed on how much the farmer would save once they'd put the new LEDs in, or installed the new refrigerators? That's what Shackleton had said, wasn't it? 'How will it benefit me?' She thought through her well-rehearsed spiel and realised that it wouldn't work at all in this place. But she didn't know what else to say.

She turned to look at the rest of the farm and her spirits rose slightly. The farm buildings were in better nick. And right next to the weed-filled kitchen garden, was a shiny new shed. The newness of the Weatherbond steel was a stark contrast to the peeling yellow paint on the house. So these guys were happy to spend money on the farm. Even if they weren't happy to spend money on their own house.

A door opened in the side of the new shed and a man walked out. He was about thirty, a stocky man, wearing overalls that used to be white but were now all kinds of dirty and even torn in places. His hair had obviously been clipped himself with a number one clipper—he had missed some places, and he wore a scowl on his face.

Mel waved a friendly hello and picked her way through the potholes and puddles to see him.

'Hi, I'm Mel, I'm from Thompson's …' she started.

'What do they want?' The words were more of a snarl than a question and Mel immediately wanted to turn and leave at top speed. This man was far more threatening than the dog this morning. But she took a deep breath, put her shoulders back, and tried again to do her job.

'I'm sure you've seen the information from Thompson's about our new energy-saving ideas. We sent you the package in the mail a couple of weeks ago. I'm here to answer your questions—'

'No need. I don't have any. I'm not doing that stuff.'

'But you could save money too, it would be worth the investment, and …' Mel's voice rose as her stomach clenched and her anxiety heightened.

'Didn't you hear me? Not interested. I don't have time for this.' The man pushed past her, stormed into the farmhouse and slammed the door behind him. Mel stood, a forlorn figure in the farmyard. She couldn't believe how badly that had gone. This guy made Shackleton look good. A lump rose in her throat and she blinked back tears. She had to get out of there before she fell apart.

Once she got back on the road she pulled over and checked where the next farm was. She was hoping for a nice long drive to pull herself together but that wasn't to be. Hopwoods was right next door to Northfield, just a little further down the dirt road.

8

Mel sat in the car and blew her nose. Between the cold and the rejection she was feeling pretty ordinary. Maybe she should pack it all in and try out this farm on another day. But then, she was right here. What was better, to go home, dwell on it for a couple of hours and then have to come back again past the driveway that was likely to give her PTSD just driving past? Or to bite the bullet, think, 'third time's a charm' and get it over with, and then go home and collapse totally making use of the nice deep pink bath and the bottle of red in the cupboard. The rain had stopped so she wouldn't be getting wet and goodness knows what the weather would be like tomorrow. She just needed to do it. It was her job.

Eventually with that kind of pep talk she was able to start the engine again and drive up yet another dirt driveway. But this one was well graded, the hedges along the side of the driveway were trimmed, and the sheds she could see further along on the hillside looked well cared for and tidy.

Mel pulled up in her little yellow car, scrubbed again ineffectually at the mud smear on the back of her leg, found another tissue in the depths of her bag and blew her nose, and then picked up her briefcase and stepped out to knock at the door of the farm office.

The door was opened by an older man, who looked like he enjoyed his food and didn't do quite enough physical activity to account for the intake, and he had tufts of white hair sticking up from his balding head.

'Hello love, how can I help you?' he said.

'I'm Mel from Thompson's, I'm here to talk with you about the proposed environmental changes you've probably heard something about.' Mel's voice wavered, her stomach clenched, and she prepared herself for yet another rejection.

'You must be freezing, love. Come on in and we'll chat. Better yet, how about we head to the house and I'll get Dot to make you a cuppa and you can warm up.'

The man walked past her and led the way to the farmhouse. Mel followed with trembling lower lip. She was prepared for harsh but this gentleness nearly undid her. But the man didn't notice, or at least he pretended not to notice and Mel used her tiny tissue again and picked her way up the steps to the farmhouse.

The stairs to the front archway were made from railway sleepers laid in the dirt and there was a beautiful English country garden planted on each side that stretched from the garage on one side to the edge of the house on the other. The roses intertwined with each other and the ground was thick with daffodils and other bulbs giving off a faint fragrance. Mel could imagine the summer months would be full of the buzzing of bees, the thickness of fragrance, the joy of life.

Through the archway was a courtyard bordered on one side by the house, and on the opposite by the garage wall, with even more garden beds and glorious flowers around the edges.

The man opened the door and bellowed, 'Dot. Can you make us a cuppa? I've got a visitor and she's pretty cold.'

There was no answer.

'Dot?' he called again. Then turned to Mel.

'Sorry love, Dot would do this better but it looks like she's out somewhere. I'll have to make you something myself. I'm Frank, by the way.'

'Pleased to meet you, Frank.' Mel's tiny hand was engulfed in a firm, warm handshake. Then Frank continued into the house and Mel followed, looking around in wonder. This was the type of home she thought existed only in story books. The room she was brought into served the purpose of a living room, kitchen, and dining room. At one end, in front of a wall of cupboards, was a large dining table. It could seat a dozen comfortably. At the end of the dining table was a large bay window looking out onto the courtyard. The window seat was absolutely perfect for curling up in and reading novels while sipping tea. Next to that cosy corner was a set of French doors and Mel could imagine the room filled for a family celebration, children running out to the courtyard through the French doors to play in the summer sun and back in again to grab food to eat.

For the winter there was a wood-heater surrounded by four cosy chairs, and heavy red velvet curtains each side of the French doors that could be closed to block out the cold. The fire was burning at the moment, filling the room with a welcome warmth. And facing the dining and lounge area, divided from it by a breakfast bench, was a warm, homely, storybook kitchen, with a large window over the double sink looking out to the valley beyond, and a huge open pantry that Mel could imagine was stacked with preserves and baked goods. There were pots of herbs growing on the window sill to catch the sun, and copper pans hanging from the wall above the stove.

Frank put the kettle on and pulled some teabags out of the pantry. 'Tea, love?'

'Sure, that will be fine. White with one, thanks.'

'No problem, take a seat at the table and we'll see what you have to say.'

Mel sat at the table, pulled out her pamphlets and a notebook and Frank came to join her. His tea was in a large mug, hers was delivered in a delicate cup and saucer that was dwarfed in his large, calloused hands. She sipped the warming comforting tea (grateful for the care he took but frankly wishing she had also been given a large mug) and ran through her prepared spiel. Frank listened politely, slurping his tea but reserving his judgement.

'So that's that. What do you think?' Mel asked at the end.

Frank took a final slurp of his tea. 'That's all very interesting, I'm sure. I tell you what, I'll take the paperwork here and I'll have a chat to Jason about it.'

Mel was encouraged by that. At least it wasn't a flat-out rejection.

'Thank you. That will be great.' Then she had to ask, 'Who is Jason?'

'Oh, I own the farm here but Jason really runs it. He's the farm manager, if you like. So he'll be making the final decisions. Maybe you can come back when he's here and meet him. He's pretty good with these new-fangled ideas.'

'Sure, I'd like to do that. Thanks for talking to me.' Mel left a few pamphlets on the table and packed the rest into her briefcase. She had warmed up completely thanks to the wood-heater and she could have stayed in that comfortable place all day, but she was sure the farmer had plenty he needed to do.

'It was my pleasure,' said Frank, 'I'm only sorry you didn't get to meet Jason or Dot. Better luck next time.'

Outside, the rain had cleared, the sky was blue again. This was definitely a four-seasons-in-one-day kind of place, Mel thought, or maybe the sky was reflecting her emotional state. She bent to put her briefcase in the car before a final goodbye when a ute pulled up next to her.

'Here's Jason now,' said Frank.

Mel looked around in time to see the door of the ute open and a large black dog jump out.

It was Bella, and close on her heels was Jason. Yes, the same Jason from the jog in the morning. And Bella jumping all around causing her to freeze on the spot. She should have known there wasn't more than one Jason in this town. But for some reason this possibility had never crossed her mind. All the comfort she had felt drained out of the soles of her feet. She was done for. She may as well head back to Melbourne now and turn in her resignation.

Frank gave the bounding Bella a solid pat on the head.

'Calm down girl, we have a visitor,' he said. 'Jason, I'd like you to meet Mel. She's just been explaining to me all the changes that Thompson's wants us to make.'

'We've met,' said Jason shortly, grabbing hold of Bella's collar.

'Have you? You never said.' Frank frowned as he looked to Mel.

'Uh, I didn't know you meant *this* Jason.' Mel's face burned red.

'Dad, we just met at the river path this morning. Don't read anything into it.'

Jason was Frank's son? Mel wished the ground would open up and swallow her. This was just getting worse and worse.

'Well then,' said Frank his frown clearing, 'do you want to sit down and go through this stuff that Mel's brought? It looks … well … it looks interesting. You might be able to make more sense of it than me.'

Mel, didn't know where to look. Frank was Jason's father, Jason was his son and his farm manager. Jason who she'd made such a terrible impression on that he'd remembered and was holding on to his dog and not allowing her to do the normal farmyard thing she was sure dogs did. And she had thought she'd made a good impression on Frank but she could see now that he had just been polite. She couldn't face going over everything again today, she really couldn't. Not on top of everything else this morning. She looked around for a way of escape. What excuse could she possibly use?

'I'm sure Mel has spent enough time talking to you this morning, Dad. She's probably sick of your company. She can come back another day and you can tell me all about it before then.'

So he wanted to get rid of her too. This was getting worse and worse. But it did mean she could go.

'Uh, yes, I really should …'

'OK, love. We'll see you again sometime and I'll see if I can do a good job explaining your ideas.'

'Thanks Frank,' Mel shook the outstretched hand, 'see you Jason.' She waved so as to not go near the dog. Then she jumped into her car and headed out, noticing that Jason kept a firm hand on Bella's collar until she was well down the driveway.

The beautiful green fields, the blue sky, and the soaring mountain ranges in the distance didn't even make an impression on Mel driving back to her house. She was too busy focussing on her embarrassment and failure.

Well, that was a day that really couldn't have gone much worse, she thought. Even the best farm didn't give any assurances they'd make the changes. And she wasn't really sure about Frank's ability to pass on the information to Jason. Not when Jason thought she was a coward and probably an idiot too.

She felt like writing her resignation to her father. She would go home and just send it off. There was nothing she could do to make a difference here and she was totally heading to a fail on the project that had been given to her. Let alone the other assignment. What kind of undercover agent meets a farm manager and doesn't know it?

She spent the rest of the drive drafting the email in her head.

When she got home she decided to try the bath and the bottle of red before writing the resignation email. It really was a beautifully deep bath even though it was pink and there was no chance of her being interrupted—there was no one here to do that.

Sinking into the bath, she thought again about giving up. But having calmed down a little she realised that she couldn't. Her father was depending on her. And she'd only given it one day. Everyone starts slowly on a new job, don't they? She was just hoping that the damage done wasn't so great as to stop her getting anywhere.

It was obvious that she needed a new plan of attack. She couldn't just go and expect the farmers to listen to her. And it had been super arrogant of her to think she could. She could see that now.

That first farmer's question, 'What do you know about farming?' stung. She knew next to nothing about farming. But she could learn.

Maybe Emma could teach her. Someone had to. She knew how to sell things—you find out what the customer needs and you give it to them. She'd been going about this all wrong. Frank had been very nice to her but it was obvious that she hadn't convinced him of anything either. She needed to start from scratch.

To: Mel
Subject: Aren't they the cutest?

Can you see the shoes in the photo? Aren't they just so cute? There was a massive sale at H&S and I got them so cheap! I just saw them as I was getting lunch today and I had to drop in and get them straight away. The credit card won't love me but they were a real bargain, I'm telling you. Sorry it's taken me so long to reply to your email. I saw no reference to cute farmers but I'm hoping by now you've got off your butt and down to the farms, seeing as it's been a couple of days. We were just snowed under until after the presentation this morning. But I'm now totally relieved that it's over and I can do things like get lunch again.
It went well, I think. Senka's stuff came in at the last minute (after several angry emails and two phone calls. That woman!) and I gave the presentation while Tom just sat in the back. Not that he was being lazy, he just didn't push hard to take over. Which was nice.
So we've made it through another cycle. I have the shoes to celebrate. And a yummy BLAT (you know, bacon, lettuce, avocado, & tomato sandwich) and chips. And an iced coffee. I'll go back on the diet tomorrow.
Tell me about the farmers!
Evie

To: Evie
Subject: You have unrealistic expectations

Evie, you obviously have a commercial-television idealistic view of the country. The farmers here work the land and have done for at least forty years. All of them. They are all old. At least the ones that own the farms are—the ones I get to talk to. And they all sit in big farm equipment all day and then eat pies and drink beer and get fat.

That's not exactly true. I have seen some larger men, but most of them are just normal-sized men. Not attractive, not many of them anyway.

In fact, I'd say I've only seen one even mildly attractive guy while I've been here. The rest are just normal older men doing normal stuff. They spend as much time in the office doing paperwork as they do out on the farm. But the farm equipment thing is the truth. There are these huge harvesters (not using them now of course, it's not the right season), huge tractors, huge everything. They are not out there sowing the seeds by hand. I was walking down the street in Lillyford the other day and this massive tractor just casually drove down the main road of the town. No one even blinked an eye.

Your picture of your very cute shoes throws me into deeper gloom. I'm never going to catch a sale again. I'll be paying full price for everything as I make serious trips back into town to stock up before my long stints out here in the back-blocks again.

I'm going to need to do that though. Do some shopping somewhere. Because the clothes I brought with me for work are just not the right clothes for this place.

I learned that straight away with that first farm I visited. Oh boy.

I put on my normal office clothes. Normal work clothes. You know shirt and skirt and heels. Stockings. And I headed up to the first farm. I got out of the car, there was a stiff breeze and I was frozen through in about two seconds. I tried to pull myself together and stride up to the office from my car, I was feeling pretty unsure of myself so I did that power walk we learned about in communications class, and I power walked right into the biggest puddle I've ever seen. My shoe is totally ruined, the suede will never be the same, and I got a splash of mud all the way up the back of my leg. Revolting.

Everywhere I go, everyone's wearing tradie clothes. Navy pants, shirt, jumper, big jackets, and most of them had high vis vests over the top, or high vis patches on their jumpers or whatever. And Blundstone boots. And this is the girls as well, there weren't just men there. The girl at the reception in the first farm I went to was wearing basically the same thing. I felt totally over-dressed.

And there was me trying to wipe a load of mud off the back of my leg with just a tissue.

You know, I didn't really feel like they took me seriously.

But there's not much option for me to do anything else yet. I'm just grinning and bearing it. I am the boss here. Well, the boss' representative. So they will have to take me seriously. I hope.

I'm just watching where I put my feet. Because there's worse to step in than just mud here. You bet your bottom dollar.

I've seen a few interesting looking places as I run through the town to get to the river for my daily jog. I'm going to go wandering into town tomorrow and investigate. I'll give you a report afterwards. Hopefully shops are still open here on Saturdays and I can see what they sell. And they tell me there's a church fair on so I'm going to check that out with Emma. It should be fun.

Mel

9

Saturday morning found Mel scrubbing ineffectually at her suede shoes. They were definitely wrecked by the mud and she really had to find something else to wear. She did her best, using hand soap and her nail brush (she'd have to find a new one of those too) and was just sitting them out on the veranda to dry when Emma walked up.

'Are you ready to go?'

'I'll just grab my bag, give me two ticks.' Mel found herself unreasonably excited by the thought of the church fair. It was the first social activity (except for the odd coffee with Emma) that she'd had since arriving in this tiny town. Even if the whole thing was a disappointment, at least she had got out of her house and met people.

'Isn't it a gorgeous morning?' asked Emma.

It was true. The last few days had been wet and windy but, fortunately for the fair, this day had dawned with a blue sky and high wispy clouds, and a very gentle breeze filled with the gorgeous scent of newly-opened flowers.

'I was so glad of it when I woke up this morning. I mean, I would have taken Gypsy out anyway, but it was so much easier when the sun was shining.'

'Gypsy? Who is Gypsy?' Mel felt an unreasonable pang of jealousy. She thought that Emma had put the day aside for her. But she'd got up early to take another friend out first. Mel was feeling like an also-ran.

'Gypsy is my mare, remember?' Now it was Emma's turn to look hurt. 'I told you about her.'

'Oh yeah, so you did. Dressage, wasn't it?'

'Yes, are you sure you don't want to join me one of these mornings? You could ride Daisy. She's pretty gentle.'

Mel had thought a little about the riding idea. Exercise, that was necessary, but riding? Horses were huge. You were so far above the ground. There was so much height to fall and so little to hold on to. She shook her head.

'I'll give it a miss. The closest I've been to riding a horse was probably one of those kiddy things in the supermarket. I wouldn't know where to start.'

'It's not hard. You just have to get to know them. And they are such beautiful creatures. I just love horses. All animals really.'

'Well, that makes sense I guess. Especially as you want to be a vet.' Mel was changing the subject. She had the feeling that if she wasn't careful Emma would keep badgering until she found herself on a horse and just the thought of it gave her weak knees.

'Maybe I'll just settle for getting medals at the dressage. I don't know how I could leave Gypsy for years of uni.'

'You'd come back for breaks and things.' Mel didn't want to push too hard but it was so awful to see this young thing giving up on her dreams. Surely she could see that a small push through would be worth the effort.

Speaking of effort, 'Will there be coffee at the fair?' Mel asked, 'I'm not sure I can last without some.'

'We...ell there's a café tent there but they only serve instant,' Emma said reluctantly, 'They serve great cake though.'

Mel shook her head.

'Maybe we can drop by the café first and get take away.'

'Mummy's? Good idea. It means you'll have to walk a bit more—the church is just a block over that way.'

'Worth it for the coffee. Unless you're too tired after your riding this morning.'

'Yeah, nah. No worries. I have plenty of energy left.'

The girls crossed the river over the arched pedestrian bridge and traipsed up to Mummy's. It seemed several other people had had the same idea about the coffee and the two girls joined the line to order behind a tall, broad-shouldered man with a thatch of dark hair that was going grey at the temples, wearing the navy blue uniform that indicated he was a policeman.

'Hi Graham, you heading to the fair?'

'Of course, but coffee first, you know.'

'They're going to have to get a coffee van or something up there. We're not into instant anymore.'

'That's for sure. Who's your friend, Emma?'

'Oh, sorry. This is Mel, she's just moved here from Melbourne. Mel this is Graham, he's our local cop.'

'Melbourne, hey?' said Graham as he shook Mel's hand. 'Why have you come here then?'

'Oh, I'm just here short term. Thompson's have asked me to come here and work with the local growers to implement some energy saving ideas.'

'So not a tree change then.'

Mel shook her head. 'Not for me, no. I'm really more the city type. But you do what you have to, right?'

'Right, right. Having much luck with the growers?'

'Not yet.' Mel had to admit it but she didn't want to talk about that. Not this morning. She fished around for ways to change the subject. 'How many of you are in the station for this little town?'

'Just me.'

'Just him,' Emma chimed in, 'but he does an OK job.'

'Not much crime here?'

'Not much. We work with the other towns. A few towns in the area here are manned by just the one cop and we help each other out when we need to. It works. And everyone knows everyone here and everything that's going on. If I need to know anything I just have a chat to Merryn.'

'Merryn?'

'Now I'm sure you've met her.'

Emma nodded. 'Yes, she's met Merryn. Mel works in her building when she's not out on the farms.'

'Exactly. She has an eye on everything that's going on in this town. So I just check with her.'

Emma laughed, 'You just have to listen to her and wait for her to get around to whatever you want to know.'

Graham joined her in laughing, 'Yeah, that can take some time, but it's worth it. Eventually she'll get there.'

The happy chatter continued as they moved up towards the counter to order but Mel was starting to think. The town was a tight-knit place. If something dodgy was going on here, wouldn't everyone know it? How would you hide it?

She liked Frank, and she liked Graham, she liked Emma and Merryn, but if they were all in whatever it was together, how on earth would she be able to tease it out?

But then, on the other hand, 'listen to Merryn,' they said. Maybe that was the next step in this interesting adventure. Maybe she should get a coffee with Merryn next time.

Coffees in hand, the three of them wandered up the hill to the church. As they got closer Mel could hear the sounds of a brass band floating towards her on the breeze, and the sound of happy people, and … was that … a rooster?

'Is that a band I hear?' she asked Emma.

'It's the school kids. I was part of the band when I was in high school.'

'What did you play?'

'Clarinet. Not my proudest moment.'

'No, no … clarinet is cool.'

'No Mel, it's not.' Graham said laughing. 'But it's nice of you to pretend. And I'm sure you did a good job of it, Emma.'

'Well … let's just say I was quite happy to put high school behind me. But Mrs Robb and I are still talking.'

'Aren't we all happy to put high school behind us?'

Graham left the two girls as they got to the fair, he was going to do some rounds of the whole place and be seen. Mel and Emma were going to take the more scenic and slower path.

The fair itself was a happy collection of tents and stalls. Mel saw where the rooster noise was coming from as soon as they entered the front lawn of the church. There was a petting zoo—lambs, chickens, ducklings, rabbits, even a ferret or two kept on a leash, and a miniature pig, all surrounded by hay bales and a small fence. There was a steady crowd of excited little children reaching through the fence to pat the soft feathers of the birds and the bouncy wool of the lambs.

Right next to that was a couple of shetland ponies for pony rides. Emma had a chat to the lady organising, all about the ponies, how stressed they were (or weren't) and how they went in the transport and so on. Mel tried to be interested but she was much more interested in the line of children jumping up and down and wiggling excitedly as they waited their turn. Some had rainbows and stars painted on their faces, some were painted like Spiderman or had tiger stripes. And some just had the blue stain of fairy floss around their mouths showing that the inability to stay still was due to a sugar high as much as anything else.

Eventually Mel got bored. Emma had stopped talking with the horse people and started talking to the people running the petting zoo. She was so interested in the animals, in every little detail. But Mel started to feel as wiggly and skittish as the children waiting in line. She decided that whether Emma wanted to or not, it was time to move on.

'I'm just going to have a look around,' she said when the slightest break in conversation presented itself.

'Sure!' said Emma brightly, so involved in what she was saying that she didn't even think she might be being rude.

'If ever there was a girl who should be a vet, Emma is that girl,' muttered Mel to herself. She passed by the book table, brushing an eye over the titles that were available. Nothing really caught her eye but she picked up a couple of books that might help her to while away the long lonely evenings in her big house with no internet access. Then she saw a stall that was much more suited to her. The clothing stall. That was far more the thing.

She was browsing through the dresses hanging on the rack when she saw someone else she recognised. Or rather she was seen by Merryn.

'Mel. There you are, dear. Good to see you. How are you settling in? Emma brought you today? She's a dear girl. Good of her to take the hint and look after you. Lost her at the petting zoo have you? Well, that's just like her. Much more interested in animals than human beings. Talks to them more easily too. Have you found yourself anything to wear? I should think you'd do better in moleskins and Blundstones than in your lovely skirts and heels. More suited to the city streets I should think. Though those high heels they do damage to the concrete even, I hear. Goodness knows what they are doing to your feet. But the farmers, they'll take you more seriously if you dress like you belong.'

Mel blinked, as she often did when talking (no, listening) to Merryn. The flow never stopped. She didn't want to be dragged around the fair by anyone, she preferred to strike her own path, but for now, without being rude, there was no way to get away. But at least she only had to nod occasionally.

Merryn cut short her chatter to turn to a young mother pushing a pram. 'Hello dear,' she said. 'And how's little Chloe sleeping now?'

'Oh much better, thanks Merryn, and I'll get you that casserole dish back soon too.'

'No rush,' said Merryn and turned back to Mel. 'Darling little girl Chloe, now that the reflux is under control. You can get yourself some moleskins in the local hardware store, oh and speaking of which ...' at which point she accosted another young lady who was walking past. 'Leslie, how are you going? Sam is at the shop today? Is he still not taking time off? I thought we'd solved that.'

'He's doing OK thanks, Merryn. Thanks to you. He's taking days off but today he thought he'd let the boys come to the fair instead. We'll be off tomorrow. You've been a marriage saver. Thanks so much.'

'You two did the hard work. Don't you go thanking me.' And on it went. Person after person that Merryn was catching up with, giving advice to. Marriages, babies, providing food for the needy, looking after the community and yes, even the odd bit of knitting advice.

Looks can be deceiving, Mel thought to herself. She would never have thought that the woman in the clashing hand-knitted colourful clothes would be such a trusted and trustworthy person. A real pillar of the community. The question was whether she loved her community so much that she would hide from the world the things that might hurt it.

Mel found herself a cute little vintage jacket and managed to un-velcro herself from Merryn to buy it. When she looked back up, Merryn was surrounded by a group of young children all proudly showing her their show bags full of toys. She looked totally in her element.

Mel meanwhile was ready for a snack. She headed to the little café stall. There may not be good coffee to purchase but she was ready for a piece of cake to give her energy to face the rest of the fair.

Red and white checked tablecloths were spread over small round tables and cakes were handed out on paper plates with plastic forks. Mel made her selection and then heard herself hailed by a friendly voice.

'Mel, isn't it?' said Frank. He looked out of place in this setting, his frame bulky compared to the little plastic chair he was pulling himself out of. He shook Mel's hand and then introduced her to the tiny plump woman sitting at the table with him.

'This is my wife, Dot. Dot, this is Mel. She's here to help us farms do our jobs better.'

'Sit down, love,' said Dot, 'come and join us. After all, a friend is a stranger you haven't met yet. Or was it the other way around?'

Mel sat in the proffered chair and Dot moved plates around on the table until there was room for Mel's huge vanilla slice.

'How are you finding the place, love?' Dot asked.

'It's very different to the city,' said Mel, 'but I think I might be getting used to it.'

'It's hard, isn't it? I remember when I moved out here with Frank. I mean, I hadn't been living in Melbourne or anything, but still even from Hobart this was a bit of a change.'

'How long did it take you to adjust?'

'She's still adjusting,' laughed Frank. 'You should hear her whinging about the lack of footpaths, and there's far too many spiders.'

'Now, that's not fair,' said Dot. 'I wouldn't go back to Hobart now. I have far too many happy memories. Have you been here long, Mel?'

'A couple of weeks.'

'Oh no, I meant to the fair. Did you come today on your own?'

'Emma came with me but she got stuck at the petting zoo. I got a bit bored listening to all the animal talk, to be honest, so I decided to have a look around myself.'

'Once you get that girl started on animals, you can't stop her,' said Frank.

'She said she wanted to be a vet,' said Mel.

'She'd make a good one. If we could get her to go to uni. But she's too scared to head out ...'

'There's no pleasing you, Frank,' said Dot. 'You don't want me to leave, but you don't want her to stay. What's good for the goose is good for the spring chicken.'

'Totally different situation. As you well know, Dot. She's at the beginning of her life ...'

'And I'm at the end of mine. Well, thank you.'

Frank looked at Mel, sighed and rolled his eyes, 'What can I say?'

Mel giggled. These guys were a hoot. They were obviously in love with each other, even 'at the end of their lives'.

'So what did you find?' Dot wanted to know.

'I've found this gorgeous vintage jacket, and a couple of books.' Mel pulled the jacket out of her bag to show it off.

'I recognise that jacket.'

'Was it yours?'

'Oh no, not mine, I was never that fashionable. It belonged to Merryn back in the day.'

'No way!'

'Isn't it wonderful how we, you know, rub each other's shoulders like that?'

'Rub each other's shoulders?' Mel folded the jacket back up and packed it away.

'You know, you rub my shoulders ...'

Frank laughed, 'You scratch my back and I'll scratch yours.'

'Yes, that's it. That's the one.'

Mel joined in, 'What goes around comes around?'

'Everything old is new again.'

'A fool and his money are soon parted,' said a new voice. 'What are you all going on about?'

Frank looked up.

'That was a bit rude Jason—are you calling Mel a fool for buying herself a jacket?'

Jason turned red and shook his head, 'Sorry Mel, no offence meant.'

'None taken,' smiled Mel.

'Just joking,' said Frank. 'We're talking about your mother's wild and wonderful sayings. Have you got yourself some cake? Come and join us.'

Jason pulled a chair over from another table and the three others squashed together still further to make room for him.

'Seen Bob or Alma today, Jason?'

'No Mum. Pretty sure they're not coming. I saw Angus turn up in his ute but they weren't with him.'

'It's not that easy for Alma to get into the ute these days,' said Frank.

'Well maybe that's why they're not here,' said Jason. 'Angus just couldn't be bothered bringing them. Couldn't be bothered breaking out the car.'

'Such a shame,' said Dot, 'they loved the fair. They came every year. Maybe we should bring them next year.'

'You'd have to get past Angus first,' said Jason, digging into his carrot cake. 'And he's not going to say yes to anything, is he? I don't even know why he's here. He doesn't look like he enjoys it. Just hangs around like a black cloud making everyone else more miserable.'

'Now Jason, I know you don't get on, but there's no need for that. Angus has as much right to be here as you do.'

'Didn't say he didn't. Just wish he'd enjoy himself a bit more.'

'Anyway, let's talk about happier things. You two should chat about those changes Mel wants us to make,' said Frank. 'I tried, Mel, but I didn't do a very good job I think.'

'Oh not today,' said Dot. 'Today's not a day for business. Jason should just take Mel around and show her the fair properly. Emma was going to, Jason, but she got stuck on the animals. Like usual.'

Jason wiped his mouth with a napkin. 'Sure, I'd be happy to show you around.'

'Only if you've got nothing better to do. I'm sure I can check things out by myself …'

'A fair is no fun by yourself,' said Dot firmly. 'No, you two go ahead and have a look around. I'm going to check out the seedlings, Frank. You can come with me.'

Frank saluted. 'Yes ma'am,' he said with a grin.

As they walked away Jason smiled. 'You think Dad's the boss but it turns out that Mum is the one that's really in charge.'

'You're lucky to have a mum like her,' said Mel as they wandered off in the other direction.

'She's not a bad duck, really.'

'She's wonderful.' Mel realised she'd been a bit strong in her response. A bit overenthusiastic. But she had been taken by surprise by the depth of her response to this lady. If she'd had a mother like that, how different would her life have been? Someone who cared. Someone who enjoyed your company just for the sake of it. Someone who looked out for others. And that reminded her, she wanted to ask.

'Who are Bob and Alma?'

'They are Angus's parents. On the farm next door to ours.'

'I didn't realise there was anyone else on that farm.'

'Well, you won't see them these days. Bob can't do anything much now, he's totally crippled with arthritis. He just wasn't able to cope with the farm work anymore, that's why Angus took over. Not that I think he's doing much of a better job. And poor Alma, she's always been stuck in that house cooking and cleaning and looking after everyone. And now she's got dementia. Can't remember anything much. I reckon it comes from overwork. From being bossed about by Bob and Angus. She'd do well if she could go into a home. But she's stuck there in the house. Angus doesn't make their lives any easier.'

'Doesn't sound like a good situation.'

'Trust me, it's not.' Jason kicked a rock. 'I didn't really ever get along with them but no one deserves to be treated like that. Every time we try to help we get kicked out by Angus.'

'Glad it wasn't just me then.'

'You got kicked out?'

'Sure did. He gave me very short shrift.'

'Well, that's not unusual. Don't feel singled out.'

'Thanks, that makes me feel a bit better.' Mel realised, belatedly, that something was missing. 'Jason, where's your dog?'

'Oh Bella's at home. I like to take her places, but you know, she can get a little excited sometimes, and here is not the best place for her. Too many yummy smells and exciting small people.'

Mel looked around at the sound and activity all around them. 'I guess you're right. It's a little distracting, isn't it?'

'I haven't seen you jogging again. Don't tell me it's because Bella scared you off.'

Mel grimaced. 'Yeah, it is, a bit. I'm just not used to dogs like her, you know? I feel like a wuss, but ...'

'How about if I promised you to keep her on a lead for the next few days? That way you could get in a jog and get used to dogs at the same time. If you're working on the farms, you need to be able to deal with dogs—they're everywhere here.'

That was true. Mel should have thought about farm dogs, working dogs. She really needed to pull herself together.

'Would it be too much of an imposition?'

'To have her on the leash? Nah, she needs to learn good manners. She's just a puppy still but it will be good training for her.'

'Well, thanks. That would be great. Meet you at the bridge at seven Monday morning then?'

'Sounds good to me. Now where will we go first today?'

Mel felt her shoulders relaxing. It was a good day with good company. There was a new emotion making itself felt, a warmth in her belly, she was content.

They wandered around the fair, looking and laughing. Every second step seemed to be an introduction to some grower or other, and Mel realised that Jason was doing her a great service. Now when she went to the farms it would not be a cold call. And she had an excellent memory for names and faces—which was coming in very handy now. Everyone she met was tucked away in the filing cabinet in her head.

There was Hector Rush, his farm was called Dewpenny which Mel thought was funny considering pennies due. But apparently the name came from England somewhere and was a very old property.

Fred Walker had been farming forever too. And Lebrina was the name of his farm, taken from an aboriginal word meaning house or hut. It was a small settlement once but the family had grown it to cover a good acreage and he was proud of it. His boys were on the mainland right now but he was hoping one would come back. 'Just like you, Jason,' and take the farm on when the time was right.

Arthur and Pamela Brown were another friendly couple. They had brought the grandchildren to the fair so the conversation was completely distracted there but at least Mel got to say hello. Their farm was called Brickhouse Farm.

Putting people's faces to farm names that Mel already knew gave the whole project a new light. Mel wondered, if her father was so concerned about the growers, whether her office mates or people from Melbourne should just come down and meet a few. She was sure it would make the processing of orders or customer questions and complaints a much more pleasant business.

The fair was a friendly place, a kaleidoscope of colour and light. But Mel was also aware of little patches of darkness around the edges. Maybe she was being over sensitive but she was here to find out what was going wrong and she kept thinking she could see ... well ... honestly, she would have thought they were drug deals if she was in the city.

Little groups of people joining and then leaving, looking furtive, looking miserable. And always on the edges, beside the hall, behind the marquee.

'What's going on there?' she asked Jason at one stage.

'What? Where?'

Mel was hesitant to point.

'Down near the corner of the tent.'

'There shouldn't be anything happening there. What are you talking about?'

'Well, those two blokes, and the girl coming up here now, she was just down there, and that kid over there in the hoodie.'

'I don't really get what you mean ...' Jason looked puzzled.

'Well, who are the two men down there?'

'You don't want to get to know them. They're the Swanson boys.'

'Hardly boys.'

'It's a moniker that's stuck since high school. They are friends of Angus's. Or as I like to think of them, Angus's thugs. They did his dirty work in school and they still do now.'

'What sort of dirty work?'

'In school? It was the Chinese burns, the beating up, the stealing of the lunch money.'

'And now?'

'And now Mum would tell me I'm being supercilious but she'd mean supersensitive. They just work at Northfield. That's all.'

'I think Angus and his thugs throw a bit of shade here. They are a miserable presence at the fair.'

'They are. So forget them. Leave them to whatever they are doing. They don't even know how to have fun. And speaking of fun, do you want to come to the pub tonight?'

'Um …' Was Jason asking her on a date? That was a bit soon, wasn't it? Not that she'd mind, too much, but …

Jason looked like he'd read her mind and jumped in quickly to explain.

'Yeah, I mean … I don't know what you do in the evenings, you might be busy, but there's a gang of us that hang out at Sal's fairly often. After work drinks, Saturdays, and just whenever. There's often a band. You might enjoy it.' Jason shrugged. 'I just thought I'd ask.'

'Oh, great.' Not a date then. Good. Probably. 'Thanks for asking. Yeah, my evenings have been a bit slow. Especially compared to life in Melbourne. I'd say I'd check my calendar but I know there's nothing in it at all. So yeah. I'll come down. Sal's? Thanks.'

'You know where it is?'

'I'm not likely to get lost in a town this size.'

'True.' Jason laughed. Mel relaxed again and told herself to stop imagining things and just enjoy the day.

I've had a great weekend. The church fair was on and it was much more fun than you would think. There were all the animals and such. I patted a cow. Then I found somewhere to wash my hand asap. But hey, I patted it. I bought myself the cutest vintage jacket. Turns out it belonged to Merryn (she of the knitted flowery jumper and hairband) in her heyday. So I may yet become an unfashionable disaster. I guess we shall see as time goes on.

And I spent some time wandering around the fair with Jason. He left his dog at home. If it wasn't for the wonder-dog I could really get to like Jason. We chatted about all sorts of things. He went to uni in Melbourne—business management and something ag-related. He says he wants to apply it all to the farm but he has to explain so much to his Dad first. Though I can't really see that being a problem. Frank (his dad) is the nicest old bloke. And his mum is just lovely. A bit dippy but lovely all the same.

After I left the fair I went to the hardware store. Merryn had told me to go there and look for clothes more suitable to the countryside. Yes, in the hardware store. And yes, taking advice from Merryn. I don't know what's wrong with me, but she seems to have some magical influence. Everyone here takes her advice, and today I joined them.

And in the hardware store I found some clothes. Clothes that suit this place. I couldn't try them on, of course, no fitting room in a hardware store, but I bought myself some moleskin pants, some boots, a couple of shirts (though I might wear the shirts I brought with me—they are more fitted than the sacks I bought today) and a decent warm jacket.

So with that and the books and the vintage jacket I've had a good day. But don't worry, I didn't buy myself a crocheted tissue box holder. I'm not that far gone. And I didn't see any at the fair anyway. The craft stuff was pretty amazing, the art that's produced in this place is incredible. Maybe they have more time to be creative, more time to think. I guess I'll have to ask Merryn about that. She'd know.

The other good thing that came out of today was that Jason asked what I did in the evenings. And the answer was, of course, nothing. I've been reading books and having long lazy baths and then going to bed. It's been pretty boring, to tell the truth. So Jason asked me out to dinner. Not a date, mind you. Don't get excited. But he said that I might like to get together with a crowd at Sal's. Sal's is the local pub. So I might give it a go tonight.

So yeah, I guess I'm settling in. But I'm not settling down. I'll be back as soon as I can.

Your countrified friend,

Mel

For all her upbeat email to Evie, Mel had to admit to herself that the butterflies in her tummy were pretty hefty ones as she walked down the hill from her house to the pub. If she didn't calm down a bit she wouldn't be able to eat anything for dinner.

But it was all so unknown. What if she was dressed too casually? What if she was too dressed up? She'd decided after a bit of looking at her wardrobe and musing that she'd wear jeans and a nice shirt with the big glass bead necklace and a pair of black court shoes with a tiny heel. Sort of upper-casual. But what if everyone else was in sneakers?

'They'll just have to take me as they find me,' she thought. There was nothing else she could do. There was no one else she could be.

And then there was the other question. Had Jason just asked her to distract her from whatever the dodgy activity was at the fair? He was pretty quick to gloss over the Swanson boys. Did he know something he didn't want to share? Did he really want her to go to Sal's tonight? Was he regretting his invitation?

The streets were empty as she walked down in the twilight. This was something she wasn't getting used to. Where were all the people? She looked up and saw a man crossing the river on the footbridge. He was heading towards her. He was probably in his fifties, just your normal middle-aged, middle-class kind of guy. But her stomach twisted. What if he wanted to try something? There was no one here to protect her, no crowd to stop him from grabbing her and dragging her away. She felt so unsafe. She grabbed her handbag with a firm hold and tried to remember the self-defence moves she had seen in a movie once.

She arranged her face to look pleasant but uninviting, or at least that's what she hoped she was expressing. Maybe it looked more like a death-rictus. The man came closer.

As he walked up, he nodded to her and said, 'Good evening,' as they passed within two feet of each other. And that was that. Mel breathed out. She would never get used to this place.

Once she had crossed the footbridge herself and walked through the RSL rose garden she could see the friendly door to Sal's. Light and music pouring out to greet her. Her spirits rose.

The sign on the door said, 'Lift your feet, you're in the country now.' She carefully stepped over the raised doorstep. Though why it should be there she didn't know. Was it to keep the ants out? The possums? It didn't seem to have any useful purpose but she was 'in the country now' so she had to learn the new country ways.

There was a long bar and bar stools on one side, and booths on the wall opposite. In between were a couple of round tables. It certainly wasn't a crowded room but most of the booths and tables were occupied and people were standing at the bar. Mel stood uncertainly, not knowing what to do. Then she saw Jason's face through the crowd. He smiled at her and for a minute her heart stood still. She waved and went over to join him.

'You came,' he said half reaching out his hand, then pulling it back quickly.

'Anything is better than another boring evening at home,' she joked as she looked around the room. 'This looks much better.'

'Let me introduce you to everyone,' Jason waved at the others in the booth. 'This is Graham, our cop.'

'We've already met,' said Graham. 'Good to see you again.'

Mel nodded.

'And this is Jo and Henry.'

'Nice to meet you.'

'I knew we'd meet sometime,' said Jo. 'We work in the same building. But you've always been out when we've been in and vice versa.'

'We're the hearing people,' said Henry.

'Oh right,' said Mel putting faces to labels. 'I'm glad we've finally met.'

Jo made a space for Mel on the booth seat and Jason offered her a drink.

'Gin and tonic?' Mel asked without thinking, and then, as Jason left, she suddenly wondered if she'd done the wrong thing. What were the others drinking? Was it more of a beer town? Should she have gone for something less girly? But though the men all had beer, Jo had a glass of white wine. Again, she thought to herself that she should be herself and not try to be anyone else.

'It's nice to have another girl to join our little group,' said Jo. 'Emma comes sometimes, but she's so young, you know?'

'She's lovely, but I know what you're saying.'

'So we can cosy up together and chat about girly things. Especially when these blokes get started on the footy. I'm really over it. Though you come from Melbourne, right? You'd probably be into it as much as these blokes are.'

'Well … only when the Demons are going well. Otherwise …'

'That shouldn't be a problem then,' said Graham.

'Ouch! We're not that bad,' said Mel and joined in the general laughter.

'Now don't get started. Surely there's something else we can all chat about.' Jo was playing at being unimpressed, but she'd brought up the topic of conversation.

As Mel relaxed into the fun chat she noticed that the music she had been hearing was live. A stage area set to the rear of the room held a small musical group—a singer, a guitarist, and a person sitting on a box and hitting it.

'Who is the group?'

'You like them? They are our very own local sensation. Amy with the sweet voice, Max on guitar, and Jude on the cajon.'

'The what?'

'The cajon. That's what they call that box he's drumming on.'

'Very clever.'

Jason brought back her drink and placed it in front of her.

'What's clever is Judd and Sarah's vision for this place. Every other pub in the town is overrun with pokies. People just sitting there plugging in their coins and pulling the lever. But Judd and Sarah decided that this should be more like an English pub. Like the ones that Judd was chef for over in England. So they banned pokies and now, well, you can see how popular it is. People love to have a place just to hang out.'

'And the food is good,' said Graham.

'Very good.' The rest of them agreed.

'Speaking of which …' said Henry.

'Give Mel time to have a drink first,' Jo objected.

'There will be plenty of time. Judd's going to be slow tonight, look at the crowd. Let's order.'

To: Mel
Subject: Seriously?

Dearest Mel,
Moleskins? Really? You are going to have to send me a photo. I can't
believe that you would do that. Surely it's better to wear clothes that allow
people to take you seriously.
We had the best time this Saturday. The girls and I. We missed you, of
course, but it was Senka's birthday and there was this pop up happening.
On the vacant block near the theatre. You know the one? It was an ad for
the latest Marvel©.
They had done this whole sideshow alley thing. All the different whack-a-
mole and then the shooting the ducks, all the old-fashioned games. And
there was this house of horrors thing. And the fairy floss and Dagwood
dogs and all the everything. It was like going back to our childhoods. We
spent hours there.
Then we went to that cosy little pub which does those amazing curly fries
with the aioli. You know, um, can't think of the name. But we went there
for Sam's promotion celebration. I'm sure you remember. And we just
stayed there all night. So fun. I haven't had a day like that in ages.
I pretty much slept all day on Sunday. And here I am, bright and early
Monday morning back in the office. Hip Hip Hooray. I really need a
sarcasm font.
Sounds like your little town isn't too bad after all. That's good to hear.
You'll survive for a few months in the wilderness and then you'll get back
to a normal place where they wear normal clothes and eat normal food.

Hang in there,
Evie

10

Monday morning dawned cold and miserable. Mel opened one eye when the alarm went off, heard the rain pounding on the roof, sighed and rolled over for another half-hour's sleep. She dragged herself out of bed, eventually. Showered and dressed in the moleskins and jacket—whatever Evie thought, at least she'd be warm today. And made herself a coffee.

As the first taste of the liquid hit her tongue she remembered. She was going to jog with Jason this morning. She had completely forgotten.

She looked out at the rain. Surely he would have given it a miss today too. No-one was dedicated enough to run through this. But, even as she looked, he ran past her house, the dog leash dangling from one hand as Bella ran along, now in front, now behind.

Her stomach sank. What must he think of her? They had a date, he'd gone out of his way to tether the animal, and she had let him down. How long had he waited out there in the cold for her? She'd be lucky to have any conversation at Sal's now. Crap.

How could she apologise? Should she head around to his house? No, that was way too familiar. And she didn't have his number, did she? Maybe it was in the records for Hopwoods, but she could only remember seeing Frank's name there. And she wasn't going to ring Frank to apologise.

How embarrassing.

What a way to start the week.

But the day was to get worse.

She arrived at her office, dumping bag and keys on the desk then looked up to see, right at face height, the biggest, hairiest huntsman spider she had ever seen. She didn't mean to, but she screamed. It just poured out of her.

And then she started to look around the office for fly spray. One eye on the spider to make sure it didn't move, and one hand gingerly patting along shelving and opening cupboards. But there was nothing there.

She called out for help but there was no answer.

She would have to go looking. There was no way she could share an office with that. And no way on earth she could squash it herself. Even the thought of spraying it was turning her stomach. It would run, she knew it would run. And where would it run to? And how would she stay away from it while still knowing where it was? The office was too small for these kinds of games.

'Henry? Jo?' she called again, her voice shaking.

'What's wrong dear?' came the response. It was Merryn making her slow way up the stairs.

'Can you get me some fly spray? Do you know where some is?'

'Fly spray?' Merryn entered the office and saw what Mel was transfixed on. 'Oh no. No need for that dear.'

Then, to Mel's great astonishment, horror, and fascination, Merryn reached over and plucked the huntsman off the wall with her bare hands.

'They're not poisonous you know, dear? You just need to treat them gently. The bite can sting but if you don't scare them, they won't bite you.'

She offered the spider to Mel, 'Want to try and hold her? You'll be quite safe.'

Mel backed into a corner, 'NO … no thanks Merryn. Not for me.' She gagged at the thought.

Merryn smiled gently.

'I'll take her outside then. Really, there's no need to worry.' And she made her way back down the stairs.

Mel fell into her chair. Just how bad was this day going to get? Maybe she should go back to bed. Start again tomorrow.

She heard the tinkle of the doorbell downstairs and Merryn came up to see her again.

'All done dear. No need to worry.'

'Thank you. That was amazing.'

'Oh truly nothing. Like I said, they can't hurt you.'

Mel just shook her head. She couldn't explain. It wasn't that she was scared of being hurt, the creature was just so gross. So hairy and terrifying. But Merryn obviously didn't see all that.

'Are there many of those things around here?'

'Oh you'll see a few. If you get one in your house, just give me a call and I'll come and move it for you. I can't bear to see one dying when it's just no threat at all. Just call me.'

Mel shuddered, but agreed. She couldn't see herself moving or killing a spider like that. But she also vowed to buy herself a good strong insecticide for just in case days when Merryn wouldn't be around.

And right now, a good strong coffee seemed to be in order too.

As Mel drank her coffee, her quivering nerves settled, and she started to think just how hilarious Evie would find the story of her whole morning when she sent it in an email. These were incidents that neither of them had foreseen. Which just showed how clearly (or otherwise) they could see the future.

Back at the office she checked her diary and found the one appointment she had made for the day. She was scheduled in to go to Hopwoods and have that talk with Jason about the changes she wanted to make. Today. The whole weekend had put it out of her mind. Well that would be fun. Not.

Well, this was her chance to do it differently. To learn about the farm instead. To be able to ask him questions and maybe even figure out the difference between a potato plant and a lettuce. She'd have to give it a go, anyway.

She detected a distinct coolness to Jason as he met her at the office door and invited her in. No offers of the farmhouse today. No warm drinks around the fire to keep out the cold of the rain.

'I'm so sorry about this morning,' she said. 'I completely forgot.'

'No problem,' he responded in clipped tones and immediately went on to discuss the paperwork.

'I think you'll really struggle to have anyone join you in this initiative. I can see the environmental reason for it but some of the others, well, they're older, they haven't had that training that you and I have had. I'm one of the only university educated managers here, most of them have grown up on the land and they have their own ways of doing things. And if I'm not inclined to do it, then I can't see why they would be.'

'That definitely could be a problem but the benefits—'

'And I've been looking at your flyers and I just can't see how we could afford this anyway, the equipment is expensive and we're just a small farm.'

'Yes, that's the thing. We know at Thompson's that you can't just go out and buy this but—'

'And the other farms are small too, we're not the big properties like on the mainland. I don't think you can treat us the same way.'

'If you could just let me get a word in?' Mel raised her voice to a near shout and Jason's mouth dropped open as he met her eyes for the first time.

'Thank you,' Mel's voice dropped again and she tried to bring in a smile. 'I know this isn't going to be easy. I realise that I've started out on the wrong foot.' Both with the farmers and with Jason himself, she thought. 'I've figured out that what I really need this morning is a lot more understanding of how things work around here. How farms work. I think these environmental changes are important, for the earth in general, but I also think they can be worked to save you, all of you, money. But before I go in with my half-baked plans, I need to understand where you're coming from. Will you take the time to show me? I'll even get my hands dirty—I'm dressed for work now.'

'I had noticed that,' said Jason, smiling wryly.

'Shall we start again?'

'What, with a jog? I've already had one of those.' The smile was real now.

'Maybe we can do the jog another day. But could you perhaps show me around your farm? I want to see everything.'

'Sure, let's do that.' Jason stacked all the flyers and papers into a pile.

'Let me take those,' Mel said and tucked them back into her briefcase. Then she pulled out a notebook and a pen. 'I'm here to learn. Let's get started.'

The rest of the day felt a bit like *Through the Looking Glass and What Alice Found There*. Mel thought she was familiar with the vegetable world, she'd spent years focusing on farms from her seat in the city. But now she was seeing things from a whole new perspective. There were challenges she hadn't really thought about before, and some of the things she had believed were difficult were not. Jason's farm had methods that had been used for generations that worked more smoothly than she had thought possible.

Even if she didn't work out what her father wanted her to, she could see that she could still bring back to the business information that was worthwhile. Especially if a tour of every farm was just as enlightening as this one.

Lunch was spent with Dot and Frank in the farmhouse. Mel had suggested she head back to town and come out again later but Dot wouldn't hear of it.

'But you had no idea I was coming. I'm intruding.'

'That's here or there,' said Dot in another of her mangled -isms. 'We have plenty to share. What kind of people would we be turning away a hungry mouth?'

'I'm not exactly a starving urchin, am I?' Mel asked Jason and he laughed.

'Mum loves feeding people. We'd have people over for every meal if she could manage it.'

At the end of the day Mel trundled home in her little yellow car feeling that God was in his heaven and all was once again right with the world. Jason had explained that he wouldn't be at Sal's tonight but that the gang would be back together there on Tuesday. And he'd suggested Arthur and Pamela might be the next best growers to go and see, and more than that, he'd rung them up and told them that Mel would be around the next day for a tour.

Mel couldn't keep the smile off her face and she raced to her email that night to let Evie know what a wonderful day she'd had.

To: Evie
Subject: A great day

Evie, I had the best day today. I decided that I needed to learn more about what farming was about from the point of view of the farmers. I tell you, it's all inside-out from what I imagined. It's just … different somehow. All the numbers we see on the spreadsheets, in the databases, it's all real stuff here. Not just numbers.

I know that I'm supposed to be looking for strange happenings, incoherence, but it may be that there is no dodgy reason for the anomalies. It may be just that city people don't understand the country. This might all be a big storm in a teacup. A big worry about nothing.

Jason took me around his farm this morning. Things were a bit tense to begin with, I had made a date to go jogging with him this morning and I completely forgot. Slept in. And the poor guy, he went for his whole jog in the freezing rain feeling stood up. And I apologised, you know, but I wasn't going to beg for forgiveness.

But in the end, he thawed (emotionally I mean, I'm not close enough to him to know about physically) and we had a great time with him showing me around the farm.

He got quite protective of me I think. He didn't want me going to the bottom of the ravine where Northfield butts up against Hopwoods. Angus (who owns Northfield) is a bit of a bully, apparently, and if you get too close to his property he'll set the dogs on you. So the Hopwoods farm keeps that paddock as a bit of bush, which is cool for the local wildlife. Apparently it's not worth fighting with Angus. And I've met Angus, he's a bit of a thug. Not exactly a little ray of sunshine.

And I got to know Bella better. That's the dog. By the end of the day I was brave enough to pat her goodbye. She licked my hand (yuk!) but still, at least I'm not looking for a tree to climb every time she comes near me.

Tomorrow night the whole gang will be down at Sal's again. That's the whole gang plus me! And I'm feeling so great about it.

Things are looking up.

How are things there?

Love,

Mel

To: Mel
Subject: Be careful
Mel, so glad to hear that you've had a good day. I was getting worried that your whole experience was unremitting gloom. You're entitled to a little bit of fun.

But do be careful. Who knows but that Jason is the dodgy guy you're looking out for. Or that lady who knows everyone—if she knows everyone is she hiding the crime? Or perhaps the policeman is dodgy. I mean, one policeman in the whole town? That's a bit weird if you ask me.

Just be careful. You've only been there a short time and you don't really know what you're looking for. I mean, Jason showed you everywhere except for that one paddock which he kept a secret and you didn't ask questions? You're not much of a detective. You need to watch more murder mysteries on TV.

You're not going to like this but I have to tell you that Tom gets a little less slimy upon closer acquaintance. You know, he bought me a box of those delicious chocolates from Nellies the other day. The dark ones with the almonds and hazelnuts. They are so *yummy*. I don't know how he found out they were my favourites (he didn't email you, did he?) but they are and I appreciated them.

And he is a whiz with the books. Him and spreadsheets—they just do whatever he says. Give him a nutty problem, he waves his magic wand over the spreadsheets, and they are beautiful in double-quick time.

But don't worry, there are no wedding bells happening yet. I will stay faithful to you my oldest friend.

I'm just not going to make my life more miserable than it has to be in this horrible place. Senka is totally going off the rails. For the second time this week I've had to stop her from driving home after drinks o'clock. Is she trying to kill herself? I'm just wondering if her life is falling apart or what sort of pressure she's under. There are all sorts of rumours that Brad's going to leave her, that she can't have kids and he wants them, or that she's losing her apartment, or things. But maybe it's just the stress of working here that's doing it. Either way it's a worry.

So Tom is brightening up things a bit for me and I'm going to take it. He's not too bad to look at either.

Speaking of which, what does your Jason look like? He sounds a bit delicious. Not quite the 50 year-old fat farmer that you were talking about before. Rendezvous for morning jogs and all that. A little bit of lip gloss and some bronzing powder won't go astray, just so you have that glowing natural look.

Give me more information!

Make my life here worth living.

Evie

To: Evie
Subject: Your life worth living?!

Evie! Who is living in the beautiful big city with the shops, food, and entertainment on tap? When am I going to ever get a box of chocolates from Nellies? You are supposed to be making *my* life worth living with your emails, not the other way around. I'm the one stuck in the back blocks.

But now you ask, yes, Jason is a bit cute. A little taller than me, buff, blonde, the most amazing blue eyes. University educated too, would you believe? He says that's where he took up jogging. But he chose to come back here and manage his Dad's farm. That's why he lives in that house in Lillyford and not on the farm.

Yes, I won't mind seeing a bit more of him. It's true.

But, as you say, no wedding bells, not even faintly in the distance. For starters, I'd have to share a house with Bella. No thanks. I might be able to pat her but she's not nearly a close friend.

Oh and the dog is a border collie kelpie cross. So now you know. Imagine choosing to live here, when you could have worked anywhere. Not that it's too bad once you get used to it. Once you get used to the limited choices and the limited faces. But, really.

I feel like coming into the city to kidnap you and get you away from slimy Tom. But I shall resist. I'm sure there are better people in this world for you than him. Don't settle. I beg you.

Oh, you're going to love what Merryn was wearing today. You know, the lady who runs the shop downstairs from my office? She is amazing. I could keep you entertained just telling you about her fashion choices. Today was just a corker. She wore her normal crocs, green corduroy trousers, a paler green jumper and over that a knitted vest with penguins on it. Knitted penguins. Then on her head was a beanie that she had made herself. Another green, a different green, with knitted flowers sticking up all over it. Looked amazing. Truly out of this world.

But she had made some raw vegan chocolate treats that she brought up stairs and offered to us. I thought they might have hash in them or something but Emma told me that she's not like that. She's just a lovely old lady with some hippie ideas. Anyway we ate the treats. They were amazing! Almost made up for not eating chocolates from Nellies. So she's not a bad sort. I might have to get the recipe from her. Or ask her to make me some more. Emma and I went and got coffee and then we sat and gossiped in the kitchen and stuffed ourselves on vegan chocolate treat things. So good.

And now (thanks to the gossip) I know that there's a farmer's market once a month in the primary school carpark, and that Northfield farm was going broke but by some miracle they've turned it around (I'll need to see if we were anything to do with that. Maybe the company gave them a loan or something), and that Jason was very well liked here in school but never had anything serious going with any of the girls (though Emma seems pretty interested in *him*), and that the old writer guy who has an office next door to mine is a best seller. Seriously. His name is Clancy Trevayne and apparently he's had some huge hits. Emma tells me to find his books in the library. I might just do that.

And if I ever write that book of my adventures, he might be able to give me some help to do it.

Oh and speaking of adventures, Merryn saved me from a spider the other day. Not just any spider—a huntsman as big as my hand! No exaggeration. It was above my desk in the office and she just walked in as calm as you please and carried it out. In her bare hands.

Ugh.

I try not to think about it, but I just had to let you know.

Farmer's market is this Saturday so I'm definitely going to check that out.

I've had a good day, but overall I'm surviving, just.

Mel

11

Mel's days settled into a new rhythm. She would start with a jog with Jason and Bella, then coffee from Mummy's and then a quick check on email in the office before heading out to a new farm to continue her education.

She learned about irrigation and the rigs they used, about the refrigeration and packaging process, about the amount of time that each type of vegetable could last before it would go bad on the supermarket shelves; and about requirements for spring rains and summer sun.

As she listened she found that the farmers also became more open to her suggestions of LED lighting, how they could band together to do a bulk order and what the company would do to help them with installation and how much it would save over time compared to the fluorescent tubes they already used. And about new ways of dealing with waste that would lower the amount of landfill and actually help with the fertilisation of the farms. They discussed variable watering and targeted fertilisation. She learned heaps but she could also teach the growers a little about the latest innovations. It was growing into a good partnership.

And then to her surprise she also found that the discussion often turned to the subjects that she was surreptitiously interested in. Even without her trying.

Hector asked why he received a lower payout for his July delivery and when Mel looked up the numbers it seemed that the goods he shipped off and the goods received were not in agreement. There was half a pallet or so missing. Hector had brushed it off at the time as just 'one of those things' and decided not to ring the office. But now that Mel was there for conversation he had decided to ask.

'It might just have been a one-off or a mistake,' he said in his gruff voice. 'But if it happens again I'll be ringing, you can be sure. We can't run a business this way.'

And Mel had agreed.

Once Hector had started the conversation, Mel could open it with other farmers too. Fred had had a similar situation. And Pamela was just waiting for a morning where she wasn't overwhelmed with things to do so that she could spend the time on hold that she was sure it would take when she rang the office to talk about the two times that her numbers hadn't added up.

Mel sat at her kitchen table, hardly tasting the pasta she had cooked for her dinner, and studied her computer. The files given her by her father, and the files on record with the company, even those had not-so-subtle differences. Then when she checked the numbers given by Pamela and Hector, again they didn't add up. It was hard to see, it was cleverly hidden, and Mel dearly missed the huge monitor on her desk in Melbourne. If only she could see them properly side by side, instead of swapping between desktop views on her small laptop. Maybe she would need to print them all out.

There was definitely something dodgy going on. Her father was right. But what was it?

Was someone selling the veggies off on the black market? That just sounded ridiculous. That didn't happen here in Tasmania. Things were readily available on supermarket shelves.

Having said that, Merryn did a great trade in giving out food to needy families. Mel decided to ask her where it came from. She didn't want to accuse Merryn of anything but she really did want to get to the bottom of this.

And then there was the truck, the infamous truck that went missing and did not turn up until all of the vegetables were spoiled due to lack of refrigeration. You couldn't look into this whole saga without investigating that. She needed to find out who the driver was.

But the more she looked at that ... well, the truck had come from Hopwoods. And that was Jason's farm. If there was a centre to the dodginess then Hopwoods seemed to be it.

And that was depressing.

After a couple of weeks, Mel had been up and down the hills surrounding Lillyford so often that she knew the area almost as well as her old neighbourhood in Melbourne. The log trucks no longer left her quivering behind the wheel as they bore down upon her and sat on her back bumper. She just waved and kept driving. The dirt roads felt like more of an adventure than a death trap. And even though she knew that the cattle grids weren't doing her suspension any favours, she was beginning to feel more inclined to invest in a new four-wheel drive than to hightail it back to the tiny Melbourne streets and alleyways.

Her new favourite activity was to go for a drive, crest a hill, and stop to see the countryside all laid out in front of her. The green hills with patchworks of freshly ploughed red earth. The little collections of farm buildings in amongst the fields. The pockets of sheep and cows and horses just grazing there, minding their own business.

One afternoon, as she sat in the car overlooking the countryside, marvelling at how beautiful it looked even when the sky was overcast and threatening more rain, Mel realised that she'd had one too many cups of tea at Dewpenny when talking to Hector. She needed to pee. And despite her newfound love of the country there was no way she was going to 'go bush' in this situation. She just could not forget the size of the huntsman on her office wall and she knew that the bush, the gum trees, the leaves on the ground, these were the spiders' natural habitat. No way she was going to squat there.

Looking around she could see that she was close to the Northfield driveway. Now there was a driveway she wasn't used to. Every time she had tried to contact Angus for a talk he had fobbed her off. She had seen every other farm and grower in the district now, some of them more than once (and not just Hopwoods) and Angus was still a stand-off. He was just stonewalling her.

Well, if she turned up today, without an appointment, but needing to use the facilities, surely he couldn't turn her down. It would be her last attempt. He'd probably be a bit angry but she'd just put up with that. She could kill two birds with one stone.

She drove past the little copse of trees, then over the cattle grid into the bumpy driveway. There was the little hedge, the overgrown kitchen garden, the almost derelict house. She decided she would bypass Angus altogether and see if she could talk to his parents. She ignored the shed and the office, and walked straight up to the house and knocked on the door.

'Who's there?' came a quavering voice. 'Is that you Angus?'

'Sorry, I'm Mel. From Thompson's. Can I use your bathroom?'

'Have you come to take me away?'

Mel tried the door and it opened.

'Hello?' she called. 'Can I please use your bathroom?'

Mel walked through the door found herself in a kitchen. It was a dark room, the dirty lace curtains only letting in a glimmer of light from the gloomy outside. There were dishes in the sink and on the bench and on the table, with scraps of food left hardening on them. There was a pot of grease with unmentionable bits encased in it just sitting on the stove. The stove may have once been white but it was white no longer, and the floor crunched underfoot. And everything was covered with a fine layer of dog hair.

'Have you come to take me? I don't want to go. I want to stay here.' The quavering voice came from a tiny lady who was holding herself against the far wall like she was trying to blend in with the wallpaper and hide. She nearly could hide too, her faded hair, skin, and clothing nearly completely matched the faded wallpaper on the kitchen wall. Then a stronger voice came from the next room.

'No, you stupid cow. She hasn't come to take you away. She's come to use the toilet. Are you deaf?' Then his growl changed to include Mel. 'Pay no attention to her, she's losing her mind. Go ahead, you'll find the loo second on the left.'

'Thanks,' Mel called out to whoever her saviour was in the other room, and dashed up the hallway.

The condition of the toilet was just as you would expect from the condition of the rest of the house. Mel gingerly lowered herself onto the seat and told herself to remember that the bush wasn't so bad next time. That little copse of trees she had driven past, that would have been enough cover. And at least it would have been washed by the rain in the last week or so.

After finding a sink to wash her hands, and choosing to wipe them on her moleskins rather than trust the dog-hair coated towel in the bathroom she headed back to find the source of the growling voice.

The lounge room was dark and the odour of wet dog and Deep Heat mixed with the smell of old grease coming from the kitchen. Sitting in a chair in the corner watching the racing on TV, was a bent-over old man with white hair. Two terriers, looking just as old, sat on the floor at his feet and bared their teeth at Mel. The man had once been a large and strong farmer, Mel could tell from looking at him, but the pungent smell and the bend of his shoulders and his misshapen hands showed her that arthritis had taken its toll. He probably hardly moved from one day to the next.

'Who's there?' came that quivering voice again.

'Shut up Alma,' said the man, 'she's just come to use the loo. I told you. *She* told you.'

'You're a friend of Angus?' asked the lady.

'Hmmf, unlikely,' grunted the man.

Mel took the lady's hand and smiled at her.

'Thank you so much for letting me use your amenities. I'd better be going now.'

'Don't take me away. I don't want to go.' The lady pulled her hand away and grabbed hold of the couch, treating it like an anchor.

'Oh shut up, for crying out loud. She is not taking you away. She's not staying,' said the man. 'I wish I could put you away,' he muttered into his beard.

Mel was torn. She would have loved to stay. Not for the company, that's for sure. But just to clean the place. This was an awful place for these two elderly people to be living. Did Angus even look at it? Or did he just expect his mother to do all the work? She obviously couldn't. The man couldn't either—it looked like he couldn't even get out of the chair without help.

'It's better if you go,' came the instruction from the chair in the corner. 'The stupid fat cow can't remember anything now. And you're not going to get me coming in to the kitchen to make you a drink or anything.'

Mel gave up.

'Well, thank you so much,' she said, 'I really appreciate it.' She moved towards the kitchen door and the old lady followed her at a safe distance.

'Don't let her out, will you? She'll wander off, kill herself falling into a ditch or something, I don't want to have to go looking.'

So Mel gently took the shoulders of the little lady and pushed her back towards the lounge room. Then she turned around and nearly ran smack into Angus.

His face was volcano red and a vein pulsed in his forehead. He grabbed her roughly by the arm and pulled her out of the house.

'What were you doing in there? Snooping? Who said you could go into my house? What were you hoping to find in there? Were you going through the cupboards or something?'

'No, no I—'

'Look I've told you often enough you're not welcome here. Then I find you've been digging through my house! I don't wanna look at whatever you're doing. I don't want you annoying Mum and Dad. I don't want you poking around in our business. Leave us alone. We're fine how we are. Just go away, stay off my land or I'll make sure you do.'

'Mum, get your fat backside back where it belongs,' he yelled at his mother as she wandered out the open front door.

'You're hurting me,' said Mel but Angus didn't care. He held her arm roughly as he marched her down the path before shoving her towards the car on the driveway.

'I'll hurt you more if you come again. Stop snooping around my property. I don't want you here poking your nose into my business.'

Mel couldn't get into the car quickly enough. It took her three tries to start the engine and the three point turn felt endless but finally she made her way off the property as quickly as the potholes would allow. Once she made it onto the highway the shaking started. And the tears. Angus wouldn't have to ask her twice. She couldn't think of anything that would entice her to go near Northfield again. To be honest, even visiting Hopwoods, the next door farm, felt too close right now.

But she was wrong. She would see the property again before she was done with this business.

When she reached the café Mel once again went straight for the bathroom. She needed to wash the tears off her face and fix her makeup. She was sure she looked like she'd seen a ghost. And she wanted to wash her hands too. In fact, she was tempted to go straight home and shower— wash the dirt of the place right off her. But that was an overreaction. She just needed to drink a coffee and calm down.

She was wondering where to sit when she spotted Graham at a table. He was just the one she needed to talk to.

'Graham, mind if I join you?'

'Please. Go ahead. You're not looking really great, Mel. Are you OK?'

'I actually … I need to talk with you. Business. Is that OK?'

'No problem. Do we need to go to the station?'

'Oh, I don't think …'

'How about you just let me know what you're thinking and we can see what we need to do after that. Right now I think you need that coffee.'

'You're not wrong.'

Mel took a couple of sips of her coffee and then pulled herself together and tried to describe the morning to Graham. She described the house, and Angus shooing her off the property.

'So do you want to press charges with Angus for roughing you up?'

Mel rubbed her arm. She was sure it would bruise but that really wasn't what worried her.

'No, no. I mean, I don't think I was technically trespassing, his parents let me in. But he might see it that way. No, I'm happy to leave his place alone. But it was so awful, Graham, in the house. I've never seen people living in such squalor. It mustn't be legal. Can't we do something about it? Surely we can move them into a home or something. They mustn't be eating properly or anything.'

'That's a little more difficult.' Graham frowned. 'For one thing, the health services here are totally overrun. There's a little nursing home here but it's completely full and I don't really want to move Bob and Alma away from their own patch of land, even if we could find another place with a room or two. And, to be honest, I don't think you'd get anyone from health to even come see them. They want to stay, you see? Alma, well you could see that even with you she was scared she'd be taken away. And Bob has his TV, his dogs, and his fried chops and doesn't want anything else out of life. They want to stay.'

'I see.' Mel's shoulders sank. 'So to get the overworked health services to move them against their will ...'

'They won't bother.'

'Couldn't we even get a nurse or a cleaner in there?'

'I think that Dot tried that a couple of years back. Angus didn't want anyone there. The poor cleaner was attacked by Alma who thought she was there to "take her away" and Bob just sat in his chair and laughed at her while it happened. To him it was the best entertainment he'd had in years. It was hard to get someone to even try after that.'

'It's just ...'

'Look, I'll pop in one of these days when I'm making my rounds, just to make sure that everything is kosher. But until someone gets hurt or asks for help, there's just not a lot that we can do. I'm sorry.'

Mel sighed.

'You finish up your coffee. You'll feel better with that inside you. If I were you I'd have some cake as well. Get your blood sugar up. You've had quite a shock this morning. But you'll get over it.'

Mel supposed she'd have to, if that was just the way things were. But she wished she could change it and the memory of that little wizened face looking up at her with such fear—that wasn't going to leave her for a while.

12

To: Evie
Subject: Need lessons in embarrassment?

Hoo Boy Evie,
I don't know if I can even write this down in black and white. This is the totally most embarrassing thing that has ever happened to a person. Ever. In the world. And I've had some embarrassing things happen lately. I got home tonight, I'd had a very difficult day. I'll tell you about it some other time, but suffice it to say I needed to wash the day away. I decided to shower.
My shower is the most beautiful thing out. That's one thing about this place, it has a brilliant shower head. My shower head has never heard of saving water. Water is a thing it feels it should dump all over you in great steamy lumps. It's the best thing to wake up with and it's brilliant at the end of the day.
So. There I was, stepping out of the shower, all relaxed and pink and wrinkled and steamy. I wrapped myself in a towel and then I saw it. The biggest huntsman was on the wall, right there in my bathroom. Staring at me.
It was bigger (if you'll believe this) than the one in my office. HUGE. Hairy. Gross. Terrifying.
I was petrified. I didn't even have clothes between it and me. Just a towel.
I grabbed for my phone, not taking my eyes off it for a second. I wasn't going to let it run off and hide somewhere in my house. I just needed Merryn to come and get it for me.

101

Yes, I'm a wuss.

But Evie, these things are huge. They speak straight to my brainstem, my fight or flight reflex. And there's no fight. I am unable to do anything but just manage to stop myself from screaming. Sometimes not even that.

And Merryn just lives the next street over, and she said to call her at any time. So I called her. She said she'd just be a minute. So I sat there, in the bathroom, wrapped in the towel and staring at the horrible creature. I felt nauseous. But I wasn't going to take my eyes off him.

I hear a knock on the door, Merryn had been super quick. I didn't know someone her age could move that quickly. Turns out … well … I call out, 'it's open' because the doors are always open in this place, and then, 'I'm in the bathroom. Come quickly.'

Then the door to the bathroom is pushed open.

You've guessed it.

It's not Merryn.

It's Jason.

I sort of squeaked at him, and then pointed at the spider. I don't know. I just wanted the thing gone. And he didn't pick it up and take it outside. He picked up one of my shoes (MY shoe!) and smashed it dead. *My shoe* was covered in dead huntsman goo. So gross.

Then he scraped everything up with toilet paper and flushed it down the loo. Then, without saying anything, he left. I heard him go right out the front door. He didn't speak to me at all. Not once in the whole thing.

I got dressed. Quickly. I heard him talking to Merryn out the front, telling her not to worry, the spider was taken care of. She asked, 'Did you kill it? You don't need to kill it you know.' And he said something. I could hear the tone of voice was comforting but I couldn't hear the words.

And then, when I was fully dressed, I had to go out and face him again to see what he wanted.

I have never been more embarrassed in my life.

Also, I'm just thinking now, I wish I had shaved my legs in the shower. Damn.

Mel.

To: Mel
Subject: What did he want?

Well?
Don't leave me hanging!
What did he want?

.

.

.

.

.

.

.

.

And when are the wedding bells happening?

To: Evie
Subject: Bells schmells. Not gonna happen ever (especially now)

What Jason wanted, which he mumbled to me while concentrating on the ground like it was some French renaissance painting or something, was to invite me to dinner at Hopwoods. His parents told him I must be lonely and that I should go out and have a meal with them. The next night. Which is tonight.
Yes, that's the way it is here. People just invite you off-the-cuff. They don't worry about whether you're busy, and of course, you're not really. Not once the day's work is done. You don't have to plan for weeks and weeks to find a time when all of you are free. They asked, and I was free, and it would have been embarrassing to say no.
I could imagine Dot and Frank asking Jason why I was not coming and he'd have to explain about the huntsman and I could never look anyone in the face again in the whole town. The way it was, I couldn't look at Jason, and he couldn't look at me, and that was uncomfortable enough. But at least the incident is confined to the two of us.
Oh and Merryn, but I'm hoping she doesn't know the whole story.
What else was I going to do tonight? I mean, Pride and Prejudice is a good book, but Mr Darcy will wait another night for me. I'm not going to turn down a free meal.
Maybe I was just taken by surprise to get the invitation. But I said yes, anyway. And he said, 'Fine, 6 o'clock,' and then he hesitated. I think he was going to offer me a lift before the huntsman incident. He sort of started something a couple of times. But in the end I said, 'Um, sure, I know where the farm is.' And that was that. He left.
And now...
Now I'm worrying about what it is going to be like. I've worried all day. Every time my brain rested it seemed to reset on Jason's embarrassed face, looking away from me, not meeting my eyes. Not that I care. Of course. It's just...
You know.
And I'm sure that Merryn is looking at me funny. With a wicked glint in her eye.
I need this job done and finished, and to get back to the city where I don't embarrass myself like this.
NO wedding bells.
Mel

To: Mel
Subject: You don't embarrass yourself?

Come on Mel, remember that party at Nigel's? That was way more embarrassing than a spider and a towel. Surely.
You have to admit, you have a talent for getting yourself in embarrassing situations.
You can keep that talent, I don't want it.
But I do want a full report on the dinner at Hopwoods. This is more than a chance meeting at a church fair, this is dinner with the family. This is important.
I'm still hearing the echoes of bells...

To: Evie
Subject: I won't dignify that email with an answer

Mel nursed her little hatchback along the dirt roads leading to Hopwoods, the corrugations jarring every bone in her body and doing goodness knows what damage to the car. She passed by the little copse of trees and the overhung driveway to Northfield and she shuddered. Maybe she could talk to Dot and Frank about looking out for Angus's parents. Just the thought of the place turned her stomach.

She wished she'd asked Jason if she could join him in his four-wheel drive. It would have been much more comfortable, even with the embarrassment, even with Bella in the back seat. And it would have distracted her thoughts from Northfield.

Come to think of it, she didn't even know if Jason would be there for dinner. She had assumed he'd join them, but he didn't actually say that he would. She found herself quite disappointed at the thought that he might not, and she didn't want to analyse that too much. She should feel relieved after the massive embarrassment she had suffered but instead …

Not worth thinking about. She wasn't going to be here long enough to be in a relationship. She was just meeting with Dot and Frank to be nice and also to build that friendship that would make it easier for her to get the inside story on the farms around here and find out what was going on. She could have a nice unhurried conversation with Frank about the changes, without the pressures of the work day. She could try to figure out (on the sly) why the trucks coming from this corner of the world were dodgy.

Yes. That's why she was going to dinner. Nothing to do with Jason at all.

Only that it would be good to have him there as farm manager.

That's all.

Really.

So why did her stomach jolt when she crossed the cattle grid and saw his car parked in front of the house?

She checked her hair and teeth in the rear view mirror, looked around to see if Bella was anywhere, and then got out of the car.

Once again Mel admired the beauty of the front garden and the well maintained buildings. She turned right to knock on the arched front door using the big circular door knocker. Even a tentative tap boomed through the house. She heard Dot's voice say, 'Get that would you, Jason?' So she had time to prepare herself to meet his eyes.

Jason opened the door, staring at his shoes. This could be a very uncomfortable evening. Mel wondered whether he had told his parents about what she was now labelling 'the huntsman incident' and whether they would be awkwardly imagining her in a towel as well. But as she followed Jason through the front entrance way into the living room her thoughts were hijacked again by the beauty of the storybook house.

The most storybook thing about it was the short, comfortable, woman who was pulling the casserole out of the oven and putting a loaf of bread in to warm up. Dot was in her element here, even more than at the fair. She was the mother Mel had never had, the epitome of comfort and warmth.

She wiped her hands on a towel and bustled around the bench to envelop Mel in a hug.

'I'm so glad you could come,' she gushed. 'On a school night as well. We were going to wait until Friday and then we realised that we would all be visiting Helen in Hobart. Our daughter Helen? Did you know about her? Anyway we're taking the weekend for her birthday. Heading down on Thursday (that's her actual birthday) and having dinner then. And then we'll spend a bit of time in Hobart. I haven't been down there for so long. So, you see, it really had to be tonight. Jason, get a drink for this lovely. Frank will be with us in a minute, now, let me see, what was I doing?' And she bustled back into the kitchen again.

Mel was soon sipping a glass of red, helping Jason to set the table for four, putting all the dishes down one end, and chatting comfortably with Dot, or at least, listening comfortably to her. There wasn't much chance to get a word in and eventually her shared embarrassment with Jason melted as the conversation bubbled around her.

She heard a door open and close and she found herself tensing. Then the door next to the kitchen opened revealing a laundry and a door to outside, and as Frank strode in to the room, an excited Bella pushed past him and ran at each of them for a welcome.

'Bella, calm down. Stop that running around,' Dot chastised.

'Come here you mongrel,' was Frank's contribution as the dog slipped through his hands.

But it was Jason's quiet 'sit' that had the effect needed and Bella sat and smiled at them all with her tail wagging furiously and her tongue hanging out.

Frank grasped Mel's hand in both of his and gave a hearty shake.

'Good to see you again,' he boomed. 'Glad you're here.'

'Thank you,' said Mel weakly.

'Well, now *you're* here Frank, we're ready to go for dinner, so if you just wash up that would be great. And kids, you can sit up at the table.'

'We're hardly kids now, Mum,' said Jason.

'You'll always be kids to me,' said Dot and continued to boss them all to the dinner table.

Mel relaxed again.

This was the family she'd always wanted. Here was the mum she had never experienced. The warm, welcoming, in control, loving, nurturing mother. She could have stayed in that house forever.

'So how's the work going Mel?' Frank asked as they pushed away from the table, all completely satisfied.

'Oh, look, it's mostly going really well. I think that most of you can see that you'll benefit from the changes as much as we will. It's been really fascinating to get onto the farms and actually see things in person. Mostly it's been great.'

'Mostly?' questioned Dot.

'There's just one or two that are being a bit … shall we say … closed.'

'I reckon I can guess who that is,' grumbled Jason.

'Now Jason,' chided Dot, 'we all know that you and Angus have a sad history, but you can't blame him for everything. Mel might well be getting along with him.'

Mel shook her head. 'No, actually. He's the sticking point. He won't let me on the farm. He won't show me anything. And he definitely won't talk.'

'Well that's what I'd expect,' said Jason.

'You've got to let it go, lad,' said Frank.

'Can I ask what happened?' asked Mel, always willing to get some dirt about someone who was driving her crazy.

'Well, if we're going to go into that, come into the lounge room so we can chat in more comfortable chairs over a cup of something.' Dot began to clear the table as she spoke and Jason led the way through another arched doorway into a more formal lounge room with an open fire and cathedral ceiling.

'This place just gets more gorgeous all the time,' said Mel.

'Thanks, I made it myself,' answered Frank.

'Really? Wow.' Mel was all admiration. Frank took a bow, and Jason rolled his eyes.

'You two sit here,' Frank gestured at the couch, 'Jason, you keep Mel occupied with your sad story, and I'll help Mum bring in some drinks and nibbles.'

'Did he really make this house himself?' Mel asked as Frank headed back into the kitchen.

'Yes, yes he did. And he doesn't let us forget it. He built it forty years ago. And it's not like he did all the work himself. But he is still proud of it.'

'Well, he should be. This is a beautiful house.'

'It works for us.' Jason shrugged his shoulders and settled back in the couch.

Mel settled back herself and brought the conversation back to the farms. 'So tell me, what happened between you and Angus. I'm all ears. Did you guys grow up together? Were you childhood friends before something went wrong?'

'Wow. That would have been nice. No. We were childhood enemies.'

'Right.' No Darcy-and-Wickham situation happening here then.

'Yes, we were growing up right next door to each other. We've always had Hopwoods and his parents have had Northfield, so we'd catch the bus to school together. But we've never got on. The fact is that Angus is a bully. I don't know why, but he's never liked me. I lost count of the times I got beat up on the bus, or just punched every time I walked past him. Woe betide me if I was carrying a book or something.'

'Maybe he was threatened by your superior intellect?'

'I guess he was. He was not the smartest tool in the shed. And I guess I made the most of that. If I couldn't beat him up I could still run rings around him in my conversation. It wasn't great.'

'Didn't your parents step in at all?'

'They tried once. I remember after one particularly bad day, I was in grade 3 maybe. I held it all together until I got home and then let it all out to Mum. I had a serious black bruise on my upper arm and a Chinese burn on my wrist. Dad came home early and he got mad. I mean, it's just not how we live, is it?

'They both decided that the way to go would be to chat with Angus's parents. With Bob and Alma. Mum made some tea cake or something and they drove over there. And I'm sure Alma didn't say much, poor woman, but Bob told them that if they were raising a pansy-boy it was on their shoulders and that their Gus was just doing what all good boys do.'

'So that was that,' said Mel.

'And yeah, we couldn't move away. There's only one school. I begged to go to boarding school in high school but Mum didn't want our family to break up just yet. She was worried that no-one would end up wanting the farm, I think. And she could be right. If I'd gone to Launceston for school then I might not be back here now. I mean look at my sister Helen—she's totally entrenched down in Hobart. Once she left, she left. But I love the place.'

'You got away for university though.'

'Yeah, I did. And that was pretty much the best time of my life. And I did my agronomy and management degree and then came back here to begin to look after the farm.'

The door from the kitchen opened and Frank came in carrying a tray with four mugs and a coffee plunger and teapot, milk jug and sugar bowl which he set on the table before taking his seat across from them. Dot followed with another tray containing her tea cake, plates, and cake forks and cream. Mel had been feeling replete, like she couldn't fit another thing in. But the smell of the coffee and the cake set her saliva glands going again. She had better not visit too often, she thought, or she'd have to buy a new and bigger wardrobe.

'Where are we up to?' asked Frank, 'Did I hear you say something about your degree?'

'Yep. We've got past the fun school stuff.'

'So this continued when you both got back from uni then?'

Jason cut a generous slice of cake and offered it to Mel. Frank poured her a coffee and then waved at Jason to continue as he served the family.

'Well, the thing is, nothing had changed for Angus but I had these ideas. I was running them by Dad, and you know, you've seen what we've already implemented on the farm. Half the ideas you are coming here with we've already had a go at. And the investment has been a bit of a pinch, but we're really getting somewhere now.'

Frank took his plate of cake and nodded. 'It's good to get these fresh ideas once in a while. It shakes you up, but there's research we can follow. It's better for farming all round.'

Jason sighed and went on.

'I thought, we're all adults now. That childish stuff from school, I can get past it, be the bigger man. All that.'

Dot interrupted, 'And we're neighbours. It's better if we get along, and what we do on our farm affects them too. So we thought we'd bury the olive branch or whatever it is.'

Jason grinned, 'Bury the hatchet, yes. Or offer an olive branch. Whichever one you want. I went over to see Angus. This must have been, what, five years ago?'

'Five or so, yes,' Frank agreed.

'We knew they weren't doing well too. We could see it in the farm buildings. They were falling down,' said Dot. 'The reason, of course, was Bob's arthritis and Alma's Alzheimers and the fact that Bob was caring for Alma and couldn't work the farm. But we didn't know that then. It was so hard for them.'

'It was, yes.' Jason took over again. 'I went around and basically got thrown off the land. Angus didn't want to see me. It took, like, five minutes before he was frothing at the mouth. I had suggested that we take a look around and I could give him a hand, maybe some pointers. Hoo boy.'

'He thought you wanted his property?'

'That's what he said. That we'd always been waiting for a chance to buy them out, to take advantage of their bad luck. That we were vultures waiting for things to go badly so we could buy them out. He was pretty much spitting at me.'

'Did he physically threaten you?'

Jason thought about that for a minute.

'No, no he didn't. Though I remember his thugs standing with him.'

'Thugs?' asked Dot.

'You know, the Swansons. They are always there to do his dirty work. Always have been. Right through school and all the way through to now.

He's never without them.'

'That's a bit rich, dear,' said Dot. 'The Swanson boys work for them, they worked for Bob when they were little. They've grown up on that farm.'

'Yeah, because they were willing to do Angus' dirty work. It might look all good from the outside but it's not.'

Frank stepped in, 'We can't accuse them of things they didn't do, Jase. I know it was ugly, but you didn't get beaten up or threatened.'

'No. I didn't. But I was so frustrated. Because I really wanted to help. Their farm was crumbling into the dirt and you know, for poor Alma as much as anything. She had never done anything to hurt me. She wouldn't hurt anyone.'

'You can lead a horse to water,' said Dot, 'but you can't make them fix up their farm.'

'Exactly,' said Jason, smiling once again at his mother's choice of words.

Mel took a breath. 'I … actually … I was at the Northfield the other day and I met Bob and Alma.'

'You did?' Dot was more than surprised.

Mel grinned wryly. 'It was a case of answering the call of nature and just forcing my way into the house.'

'I bet that was an eye-opener for you,' said Jason.

'You're not wrong. I was hoping you could … I had a chat to Graham afterwards. I mean, people shouldn't live like that. It's one thing to not look after a farm, but to treat your own parents like that …'

Frank shook his head. 'There's not much we can do. We've tried, believe me Mel, that's why we were worried that Bob and Alma weren't at the fair. It was their one outing a year. But we can't do anything until we're asked. And Bob might not be as unpleasant as his son, but he's a stubborn old bugger and he won't let anyone in there to help.'

'But he can hardly move. He looked glued to his chair. And poor Alma …'

'It's a sad situation dear, but our hands are tied right now,' said Dot. Mel had to accept it.

Mel took a sip of her coffee and then frowned.

'I'm puzzled about one thing. You say the farm was falling down. But I've been there, at least I've been through the gate. The house is awful, but there's a nice shiny new shed there, and the numbers (though I shouldn't say too much) in the company records look good. At least the few numbers I've seen. I mean, it's a successful farm now. And you're saying that the brink of bankruptcy was only five years ago?'

Jason and Frank locked eyes and Dot took a good sip of her cup of tea. There was a long pause which was broken by the theme from The Twilight Zone. The timing was so appropriate that it took Mel a few moments to realise that the song was the ringing of her phone and as she dived for her bag the room collapsed in laughter. Checking her screen she saw that it was Evie ringing and she decided she could ring her back or write to her later. She could wait. She probably just wanted an update on the 'date' night that Mel was on.

The tension was broken but the question still remained and Frank suggested, 'Maybe Angus is good at running a farm. Maybe the fact that he took over from Bob and could think clearly is enough.'

'Not likely,' mumbled Jason.

'Maybe he has farming in his blood and he can just do it by instinct,' suggested Dot.

Jason shook his head and muttered into his coffee cup.

'Well, something has happened there. That's for sure,' said Mel. 'But unless something dramatic changes, I'm never going to know what it was. They just won't let me anywhere near the place. And you lot aren't encouraging me to try.'

'No dear, I wouldn't go there for a while,' said Dot. 'Concentrate on the other farms. They're treating you all right, aren't they?'

'They're not all as hospitable as you are, but they are letting me in and listening. And now that I've learned my lesson, I'm listening too and learning so much,' said Mel with a smile. Gosh, she loved this comforting woman. Being with her made her wonder just what life would have been like with a mother at home.

She took a bite of the tea cake, 'Dot!' She said with her mouth full, 'This is amazing cake. How do you make it so light and so delicious?'

'She should give lessons, I always say,' said Frank.

'Yes, he always does,' said Jason.

Frank leaned over to give his son a friendly smack on the arm. 'Don't you agree with me?'

'Yes, Dad. Yes, I do. She should give lessons. But she's not going to, is she?'

'Who would come and learn from me, when there's Merryn in town doing her thing? No, I'll just keep feeding you up, and you keep finding me visitors.'

The friendly argument continued for a while, lapsing into banter that was light and friendly. Mel sat and ate the amazing cake and drank her coffee and enjoyed the company, adding non-committal comments whenever she was called upon. She didn't think she'd had a nicer evening in weeks. In months. Probably in years.

There was none of the competition or in-crowd rivalry that was part of every social occasion in the city. There was no tension in the room at all. Bella had gone to sleep in front of the open fire and twitched occasionally like she was chasing rabbits in her dreams.

Eventually Mel stifled a yawn and Frank caught her at it.

'We've kept you up too long, and you have a drive ahead of you too.'

'I really don't want to leave, but I guess I should while I'm still awake.'

'You don't want Jason to drive you home and bring you back for your car tomorrow?' That was Dot's suggestion.

'No, no. I'm fine.' Mel wouldn't hear of it. Where would her reputation (such as it was) for being an independent woman go, if she couldn't even drive home after a dinner?

But the night was over. Jason and Mel moved to their respective cars and she followed him down the driveway and was woken up completely by the freezing night air and the bone shuddering corrugations in the road.

As she went to sleep that night happy memories chased each other through her mind. But her last thought was, 'How *is* Angus making the farm work? And how am I going to find out?'

To: Evie
Subject: It was beautiful!

Oh Evie,
Sorry I didn't answer your phone call, I was at the most amazing dinner with Dot and Frank. I've never experienced anything like it in my life! How to explain? Well, they were just lovely people, in a gorgeous house (that Frank built himself), and the food was amazing, and Dot is just so gorgeous and motherly and funny too. Hilarious things she says like 'We'll come to that bridge when we cross it'. And she said something about her descendants being buried in the churchyard here in Lillyford and the boys had to correct her on that one and remind her that she meant ancestors. We were in fits, Jason was looking at her sideways like maybe she was going to kill him and bury him in the churchyard.
Maybe you had to be there. But it was a great night. Not at all like the great parties we have in town, something deeper, more comforting.
We had a bit of a talk about work stuff as well. I'm wondering if you can do me a favour? I'm curious about the history of Northfield. Could you dig a little into old records and see if you can find anything that changed about the place about five years ago? I'd just be really curious to know. And I'm sure I don't have to remind you to keep it on the down-low. Don't tell Tom. I mean it!
I would ask the farmer himself, his name's Angus, but right now he's refusing to even talk to me. I think it's just mysogyny. The guy is a bully, and he lives in the dark ages. But I still want to know.
Anyway, it was a good night. Very enjoyable. Thought you might like the report back and all that.
No Bells!
Mel

Despite what Mel had written to Evie, she dressed herself with a little more care the next morning before her run, making sure her hair was brushed up into the ponytail, not just finger-combed. Putting on a little lip gloss. She couldn't help it, she was looking forward to seeing Jason again.

She made her way to the riverside path and smiled to herself as she heard steps coming up behind her. But then, the steps sounded different, lighter, and shorter, and there was no accompanying four-footed friend.

A puffed voice called, 'Mel, wait!'

And Mel stopped and turned to see Emma.

'Good morning, strange to see you here this early,' Mel greeted, trying to swallow her surprise and disappointment.

'You've been ... setting such a good ... example,' Emma explained. 'I thought I'd ... join you.'

'Great,' Mel forced a smile. 'But won't Gypsy be disappointed?' They set off, at a slightly slower pace to allow Emma to keep up.

'Oh, she'll be fine. I'll go out with her tonight instead,' Emma puffed. 'But you know, it's good to get some cardio fitness too.'

Even at the slow speed they were jogging, Mel couldn't have a conversation with Emma. The poor girl was puffed. And when Jason's expected footsteps were heard behind them, he just waved and called a cheerful, 'hello' as he overtook and sped down the lane. The morning wasn't going quite as Mel had planned, but she couldn't blame Emma for that.

Eventually their pace dropped to a walk and Emma started to catch her breath.

'I'm not sure this is for me,' she said.

'You'll get used to it. Truly, it's such a good way to start the day. And I can imagine that as the days get longer here it will be so beautiful.'

'Yeah, that's true. I love it when I'm riding.'

'I might have more cardio fitness than you, but I reckon your core must be so strong with all that bouncing up and down with the trotting and stuff.'

'You're probably right,' said Emma. 'Maybe I should stick with what I'm good at.'

Mel decided to take the opportunity to ask Emma something that had been niggling at her since that first coffee together.

'What's stopping you from getting that veterinary training? The more I know of you, the more I can see that an office job isn't your thing.'

'Well, you know, it's the years away from here. This is what I've known, what I've always known. And yeah, I'm in the office but the work's not bad and I can always spend my weekends and after hours with the animals. And you know, a lot of people go to the big cities and work stupid hours, and slave away for years. They work really hard so that they can save up enough, or invest enough to retire early. Then they often come back to a place like this, and work part-time and enjoy the peace and the closeness to nature and all that. Well, I already have that. I already have the part-time work. I have the peace. I have the friendships, and I live in this beautiful place. But there's no guarantee that I'd have a vet job back here if I went away and did the training. So I just stay.'

'You've obviously thought that through.'

'That's one of the benefits of living here,' Emma said with a laugh. 'You have the time to think.'

Mel couldn't help but agree. The slower pace of life, the chance to stand at her kitchen window with a cuppa and watch the birds playing in the tree outside, those little moments of peace were a major benefit of being in Lillyford. Something that was really hard to explain to people back home.

'Do you get bored though?'

'Are you getting bored being here?'

'Well, I guess I am sometimes, a little. But sometimes I wonder whether even that is a good thing.'

'Now you're catching on,' said Emma. 'You see, it's just a different way of looking at the world.'

They walked on in comfortable silence for a while, Mel mulling over what Emma had said.

Then Bella bounded down the path towards them.

'How about you leave me to recover, and jog a while with Jason?' Emma said.

'I don't want to abandon you.'

'Oh no, really. I have a lot of fitness catching up to do. I'm sure you want to stretch your legs.'

Mel did. And she wanted to chat with Jason. So she did as Emma suggested and made her way back into town, feeling totally virtuous and only slightly under-exercised.

Jason seemed pleased to be able to run with her as well.

'Thanks for coming around last night. It made Mum and Dad very happy.'

'It made me very happy too. I can die happy now that I've tasted that tea cake.'

'Yes, it has that effect on people,' Jason said with a laugh.

'It was really interesting to hear about your history, and Northfield too,' said Mel. 'I'm sure it's going to help me heaps just to have that background.' Then Mel realised she might be giving things away a bit and backtracked as far as she could. 'I mean I won't go and push it again straight away, but the bosses are going to want them to cooperate and … yeah.'

'Yeah, well, if I were you, I'd give it a miss. If Angus doesn't cooperate, then he might lose his contract. I don't want that to happen, obviously, but he needs to get some consequences for his actions.'

They had reached the end of the path now and were standing and stretching in the playground at the end of the high street.

Suddenly, Jason seemed to make a decision. He stopped everything and turned to face Mel.

'Really Mel, I'm totally serious. Just drop Northfield. Let someone else deal with it if you can at all. Angus is a dangerous man. And you don't want to get on his wrong side.'

'But, I'm a stranger. I don't have the history you guys have. And it seemed to me that you have figured out a way to co-exist peacefully anyway, haven't you? If you can get along, then … I mean, I'm just doing my job.' Not that Mel wanted to go back to Northfield, but she was beginning to see that Northfield was the key to this whole business. If she couldn't investigate, she'd never figure out what was going on.

'I'm not sure about the co-existing. I'm actually really worried about the whole situation. I didn't want to say so in front of Dad. You might have noticed me avoiding some questions.'

'I did yeah. I thought that was because of me being there.'

'No, it's Mum and Dad. I don't want them to worry. They're trying to let go of the farming and let me take over. I want them to have a restful retirement. But I'm starting to get really concerned.'

'What about?'

'I think Angus wants to put us out of business. He's not just hiding what he's doing on the farm, he's started to act—I dunno—strange, threatening.'

'You think he wants to buy you out?'

'No, it's not that. At least I don't think so. I'm not sure what it is. It's like this. I was in the pub, just last week. You know, just hanging. I don't go often. But there was Angus and his thugs.'

'Yes, I know the thugs.' Mel smiled.

'They were talking at the bar and I went up to get a refill and suddenly he's all crazy. Standing over me, telling me to get out of his business.'

'But why? You were just there.'

'He thought I was trying to overhear his conversation while I waited for my drink. Nothing was further from my mind. I do not care at all what he says or does. I wish he'd move away. But he was all, "get out of my business" and then he said, "You'll find what's coming to you, if you keep sneaking around my farm".'

'Hang on, *have* you been sneaking around his farm?'

'Mel, our farms intersect. They share a boundary. I went down a couple of months ago to check the fences. I'm not going to trust him to look after anything. And he saw me there. That's all I can think of. In fact, when I was on the boundary fence, I saw that he was ploughing up a small paddock that hadn't been used in years. I was happy. I thought he was finally taking things seriously. I don't know what his problem is. But you remember I wouldn't take you down there when you first came. He's insane and I think he could be dangerous.'

'You're worried he's going to make his problem yours.'

'He could do so much damage to us. He could sink wells and limit our water, he could plant GMO foods and infect our pastures. He's so vindictive, I wouldn't put anything past him. Even salting our land.'

'Salting?'

'Putting salt on the earth so that nothing will grow. That's what he was threatening at the pub.'

'That's a huge worry.'

'Yeah, it is. But I can look after us. I'm just keeping an eye out. Telling my workers to let me know if they see anything strange. Don't worry about us, we'll be fine. But I guess what I'm really saying is, don't you go and stir up a hornet's nest for yourself. He's not a good enemy to have. If I were you, I'd stay well away.'

Mel looked over the water while she thought about that. And saw Emma dragging herself up the path.

'Emma, come and stretch,' she called.

'What? You have to stretch too?' Emma complained, 'I don't think I'm made for this at all.'

'You'll get there. Just have a quick stretch and we can all go to the café for a coffee as a reward.'

'You girls do that,' said Jason. 'Have fun, and have a treat for me. I'd better get my backside into gear and get down to Hopwoods.'

13

Back at the office Mel checked her inbox to find an email from Sharon. She had completely forgotten about reporting back to Sharon. Her father must think she was just wasting her time here, swanning around, enjoying the holiday. She needed to check in.

But what to write? What did she actually know?

Well, she knew that the farmers were complaining about the trucks not being full. And that she really needed access to more detail from the company. And that the epicentre of the problem was around Northfield and Hopwoods.

It had to be Northfield. There was no way that Dot and Frank were going to be involved in any dodgy business. Surely not. And if Jason was, he was hiding it well.

But facts. She didn't know many facts.

And that little conversation with Jason this morning. Well you could think of it as Jason warning her for her own good. But you could also think of it as Jason trying to stop her from snooping around. Either way he was trying to keep her away from the farm. Surely he couldn't be involved. Surely it was Angus.

But did Angus have the brains to do the dodgy business? I mean, really?

What if Jason was working with Angus?

What if it was a 'good cop, bad cop' situation? Because whichever way Mel looked at it, she couldn't differentiate between the two farms. Not yet. Not without more facts.

What if it was just the truck driver? She needed to check whether the

122

same driver was involved in all of the anomalies. Had she been given the records of the drivers?

And Jason hadn't shown her the whole of his farm. He'd been forthcoming to a point, but he wouldn't take her to the border of the two farms.

But then, where did that new shiny shed come from? What was going on there? How did Northfield run?

Mel decided to ask Sharon for more information. For all the historical spreadsheets on Northfield and Hopwoods. And for the records of the drivers used for this area. She would have to do some targeted digging. And she must not let emotions blind her to the facts. If it was Jason, it was Jason.

She just hoped it was Angus.

While she waited for a return email from Sharon, Mel sat and drew up a map using the information that her father had given her, and cross referencing with the complaints she had received from the growers in the region. Every truck that had been missing some stock had either gone to Hopwoods and/or Northfield before the farm in question, or afterwards. And it was impossible to distinguish between Hopwoods and Northfield. For all that Jason talked of them being separate entities—and maybe they were—deliveries and pickups would go to one and then the other. Or even if they only went to one, they could go to the other as well. The two farms were as close as conjoined twins.

How would she tell them apart?

More to the point, how would she investigate them?

She hoped that Evie had done some snooping on her behalf. She checked her email again. And again.

Finally an email came through but it was not what Mel had been hoping for.

'Tom does the work for the farms in your area. I can't ask to check his work. I've told you what a genius he is with spreadsheets. I'm sure that everything you read in the reports is the best, most succinct reporting you can have. I've attached the last five years' reports in case you can't access them there.'

What was going on? Why was Evie not backing her up here? A friend in need and all that. Tom's word against Mel's. Well that was nothing new, was it? He must be acting especially smarmy to get Evie on side.

Having the reports was something, but Mel could see a visit to Melbourne coming up soon if she couldn't get more information through Evie. Honestly, it was so frustrating to be stuck out here, hours away.

She printed out the relevant pages of the reports Evie had sent and, for now, went on with her cross-referencing. Painstaking and slow though it was.

At the end of the day Mel's eyes were crawling with facts and figures, and the numbers were mixing themselves up on the page. She needed a change of scene. It wasn't a normal pub night with the gang but she was far too tired to cook herself something, so she decided to head along to Sal's for a cooked dinner treat anyway.

'Good evening Mel,' said Sarah. 'This is a treat for us.'

'It's a treat for me, more like it. I've just had the worst day. What do you have that I can eat for dinner to cheer me up?'

'Now there's a challenge that Judd will love. How about you just relax in the booth over there and I'll bring you something delicious. There's nothing you don't eat, is there?'

Mel laughed. 'No, I eat it all. Probably too much of all of it. A surprise meal will be great.'

'And a wine pairing. You leave it to the experts. This is what we love to do.'

Mel snuggled herself into the corner of the booth. This was what Sarah and Judd were born to do, it was obvious. What a fantastic couple they were. And they were happy being here in little Tassie. You didn't see them complaining that the village was too small, or that there was a lack of celebrities, or that Sal's wasn't getting the Michelin stars it deserved. No, they knew what they were here for—to provide good food and drink, and a cosy chatting experience—and they got a lot of joy out of providing it. She assumed they had good days and bad days just like anyone else, but they didn't seem to show it.

Although Sarah's voice did sound a little more stressed when the next guests came in.

'How can I help you fellas?'

'Beer, chips, and lots of it,' came the unmistakable gruff tones of Angus. Why was he here? Wouldn't he be better off at the other pub—the one with the pokies? Mel didn't want him to see her so she put her hand up to the side of her head while he and the thugs looked around for a place to sit. Sure enough, just like she thought they might, they chose the booth right next to hers. They would be her dining companions for the night. Just her luck.

'So Gus, what's the plan?'

'The plan, idiot, is to wait until after we get the food before we talk. We don't want anyone hearing this, remember?'

'Oh. Yeah.'

That made Mel prick up her ears. A plan? Well, maybe she was in the right place after all.

Her food showed up. A taster plate of flat breads, dips, meats, cheeses, and antipasto. Light but filling. And a Sangiovese Rosé to go with. Just perfect. She smiled her thanks at Sarah but her words of thanks were mouthed rather than spoken out loud. She didn't want Angus to know who was sitting at the next table. She hoped he wasn't observant enough to work it out.

The beer and chips were delivered and Mel was ready to hear what they were going to say. But once they got started they had the sense to reduce the volume of their conversation to a mumble. Maybe Angus wasn't the dunce that Jason made him out to be. Mel strained her ears and her powers of concentration to the utmost but it was a struggle to hear what they were saying.

And she didn't really have anything to go on either, anything past those hints and maybes and worries that Jason had laid at her feet that morning.

Well, it was a nice idea, but she was never going to be a spy. Unless … unless she invested in some surveillance gear. That was an idea. Sharon could send her over some stuff and she could bug the table and … no, how would she know what to bug? And there was no way she could bug the farm. That was definitely the wine talking. She was getting stupid now.

She held up her glass to the light. Wine was just such a beautiful liquid to drink. It looked gorgeous, it smelled gorgeous, and the taste was perfectly paired with her meal. Judd knew his stuff.

And as she was just staring at the wine she heard, 'Friday, … away then.' And as she carefully put the wine glass down, trying to hide her shock, 'Graham … Ellenworth … clear. Tell … 4 a.m.' She almost turned around and looked over the booth chair at the table. Did she hear correctly? Did they say Friday?

How could she hear more? She needed to hear more. But it was not to be.

Sarah decided that now was the time to top up her glass and sit down for a little chat and a break. Which was lovely, really it was. The timing was way off though and Mel found it hard to concentrate on the little tidbits of gossip Sarah was sharing. She was half listening, and half straining to hear more of the conversation from the next table. Still it was good to have a friend to chat with. Even if Mel couldn't say what was on her mind.

Mel had tossed and turned all night trying to process what she had heard. Trying to put all of the messages together in her head. And the more she thought about the scraps she had heard, the more she thought there was something there.

Angus and his thugs were up to something on Friday. It was something that was going to happen when Dot and Frank would be away. They were going to Helen's party. She could put those pieces together. So it was something to do with Hopwoods.

And Jason had told her that he was worried for Hopwoods, that Angus was going to salt the land, or dig wells, or do something. But she had no idea what he was going to do. And she had no proof.

What she wanted to do was organise a band of vigilantes to guard Hopwoods while they were away. But she didn't really have the clout to do that yet. The friends she had made were still tentative. She was still so new to the area. Why would they even think of supporting her?

But Jason knew them well, he could organise something. She just had to convince him.

And she could do that on her jog this morning.

That thought got her out of bed and going.

At the riverside path she could see Jason just heading around the bend in front of her. Sprinting, she caught him up and then puffing a little, hands on her hips, she tried to convince him of her concerns.

'I'm sure Angus is going to try something on your farm on Friday night when you are all away.'

He stared at her openmouthed.

'I knew it was a mistake to tell you anything.'

'What? It was you telling me all about your fears and stuff, and I overheard something at the pub. Angus talking. I just thought I should warn you.'

Jason shook his head.

'You think this is some kind of spy drama or something. I just told you to stay away from him, and there you are trying to overhear his conversation and tell me something is going on.'

Now it was Mel's turn not to believe what she was hearing.

'Look, I'm just trying to be helpful. I wasn't trying to overhear anything. I wasn't spying on your behalf. If I happen to hear something and I think it might be helpful, I'm going to pass it on.'

'This is not a game Mel, it's my livelihood.'

'I know! That's why I'm telling you.'

The two of them stood on the path, all but wagging their fingers in each other's faces.

'Look, you just stay away from Angus. That's all I was saying. I can look after myself.'

'Sure. No problem.' Mel's voice was flat. 'I'm just saying, look after yourself on Friday. Something is going down then.'

'Sure. Something is. We are. Dad, Mum, and I are going down to Helen's 40th. I'm not going to miss my sister's party just because someone overheard someone else say "Friday" in a pub.'

'You're going to be away Friday? That's what he was saying!' Bella started barking, excited by the tone of Mel's voice and Jason turned away to grab her and attach the leash.

'No, we're going down on Thursday. Staying Thursday night. Staying the whole weekend, if you want to know. You only turn forty once and we want to be there for it.'

'You don't believe me at all?'

'Sure, he probably said Friday, they're probably going to drink all night or something. You're reading into it. Just leave it alone.' Jason turned to continue jogging and Mel watched him go.

So much for that then. She had tried, but he hadn't listened.

What next? Graham? He'd need more proof than Jason. It was useless. She walked home, shoulders bowed and feet dragging.

Once she made it to the office, Mel looked at her watch. She needed to get a wriggle on. There was a work conference call coming up and she needed to be ready for it. Maybe if she could convince them that there was something dodgy about Northfield she could get some help from that quarter. Though what they could do in Melbourne to stop what was going down in Lillyford she didn't know. That's what she was supposed to be doing. That's why she was on the ground here.

It was good to see Evie's face on her computer screen again. It was less good to see Sharon's face and she could have done without seeing Slimy Tom's altogether. But that's what you get with work colleagues.

'How about you tell us how you're going, Mel?' Sharon asked.

'It's going pretty well, actually.'

Mel found that she had lots to report about the farms that had been in talks with her. She could tell the city folk what she had learned about the pressures of the farms, and the success she had been working towards with the idea of investment in energy efficient refrigeration.

'They are all onside in the area of lighting as well. They can see the benefits of a bulk order of the new long-lasting bulbs and are happy to work with us to get a contractor to change them all over.'

'So you have them all in the palm of your hand? That's great.' Sharon sounded pleasantly surprised.

'Well, almost all of them. Northfield has been a problem.'

'Northfield?' That came from Tom.

'Yes, they won't even let me on the farm. You don't know anything about that farm from your side do you?'

'I've worked with the Northfield account since they came on board with us. They haven't caused me any problems.' That was Tom as well.

'Maybe you're not batting your eyelids enough,' said Evie. 'Not everyone is ready to listen to a girl tell them what to do.'

'It could be that. I'm not convinced.'

'How about I talk with him, Angus isn't it? Angus Harmley? If I talk with him we can see if it's just a woman issue.' Tom seemed eager to help.

'That sounds like a fix to me.' Sharon was ready to move on to more facts and figures and the meeting progressed. Mel hoped that Tom was right, but she was pretty much convinced that there was something more sinister going down at Northfield. And how was Tom even going to ask about Friday? Well, he wasn't, was he? Because Mel hadn't asked him to and no-one knew that something was going on. This spy stuff was hard.

Plus there was something strange about the eager way that Tom was jumping in to help. Or maybe there wasn't. Maybe Mel was starting to see things, just like Jason thought she was. Maybe she was reading into all of it.

Well, Tom wasn't her problem, but Angus and Friday night might be. She had some thinking to do.

14

Meeting over, Mel slowly packed up her office and slipped her bag over her shoulder to make the walk back to her house. What would she be doing if she were back home? Going for a drink with Evie? Then back to the crowded train station, down the escalator into the depths of Central, squashing into the hot and smelly carriage with all the rest of humanity that inexplicably wanted to be on the very same train that she did. Then pulling herself up the steps at the station and making her way back to her studio apartment to stare at the cupboards and fridge and hope that dinner would make itself. Then usually, if she was honest, a walk back down to the corner through peak hour traffic fumes to buy some takeaway noodles or sushi and then sitting in front of the TV, barely tasting the food before falling into bed.

And instead, here she was, walking home through the fresh air. The walk home was invigorating enough that she wanted to cook something healthy once she got home. And there was time to do it too, because there was no long commute eating away at the hours in the day. After eating she was going to finish the book that Merryn had convinced her to read, the one by Clancy Trevayne, the author in the office next door. When she had left it last, the heroine was getting herself into such a pickle and it was only Mel's exhaustion from a day out in the fields at the farm that had allowed her to put it down and go to sleep.

There was no doubt, this was a more relaxed and healthy way to live. She found she wasn't missing Melbourne at all. More dreading the thought of going back there.

But it wasn't all peaches and cream here in the country, she had to remind herself. Whether anyone else thought so or not, Angus was up to something and she had to figure out what it was.

But what could she do? No one would believe her or help her out. It was just like always, she would probably have to take the job on herself to make sure it was done right. Somehow she would need to stop Angus on her own.

Evidence. She needed evidence.

She opened her door and dropped her bag on the floor and her phone on the kitchen bench. And then she stared at her phone like she'd never seen it before. It wasn't just a phone, it was a camera. And not just that, it was a video camera. What if she could get evidence of what Angus was going to do? Whatever it was. If he was doing something dodgy on Friday, he'd have to be preparing on Thursday. There would have to be some evidence hidden away in that shiny new shed. If she could get some photos or something then she would have evidence to show Jason and Graham.

Something had to be done. Dot and Frank needed to be protected, even if Jason was in on whatever Angus's deal was. Mel could not believe that Dot and Frank would be doing something even slightly dodgy. And there was nothing she could do without proof. She needed some proof.

So it was decided. She would hide herself carefully at Angus's farm on Thursday and get some evidence, some video or photos on her phone, or something that could point to him and whatever he was doing. She would take that to Graham Friday morning and Angus would be stopped. She would save the day.

Or at least do some good.

Thursday night arrived. Mel had tried in the intervening time to find some evidence of Angus's dodginess in a more normal and risk-free fashion, but she had got nowhere. She didn't even really know what she was looking for. Was he doing something that was a problem for Thompson's? Maybe it really was only the rivalry with Hopwoods that she needed to worry about. But she had hit a brick wall with the files her father had given her. She wasn't going to get anywhere without going to Northfield and looking around. And she wasn't able to do that when Angus kept kicking her off his property. She needed to go there and get evidence.

And no one else was going to do it. Jason wasn't going to help. Evie had let her down and was probably in cahoots with Tom. Graham was away and she had nothing to get him interested anyway. If you wanted a job done, you had to do it yourself. That was always the way. So that was the plan now.

And she wouldn't be in danger, not really. Whatever was happening, was happening on Friday. She had heard Angus say that. So this was just going to be a fun adventure to go and find some evidence. No danger at all. That's what she was telling herself. But the butterflies in her stomach told a different story.

She had hoped that Clancy's book would help the hours to pass as she waited for the night to become totally dark, but the imaginary danger of the heroine in the book was nothing compared to the adrenaline she was feeling with her real adventures and she kept dropping the book in her lap and staring out the window. Eventually she decided it was time to get ready to go.

Choosing her darkest pair of jeans and her grey hoodie, Mel dressed with as much care as if she was going to a cosplay event in town. Or a date with Jason should that happy event ever come about. (Not that it was likely now, after the last time they talked.) She tied her hair back and tucked it under the hood. She wore her brown boots and black socks, and thought about putting some dirt on her face. Then she really couldn't bear that thought so she just pulled her hood further over her head so that her face was in shadow.

'You're being stupid,' she told her reflection. 'This is a totally daft idea that will get you fired and destroy all your plans. Evie and Tom are right, you should stop reading mysteries, get yourself a nice soft romance, and tuck yourself under your comfy rug and just forget about it.'

Then she pulled the hood back off her face and looked herself sternly in the eye.

'Well, do you believe in yourself, or not?' This was the hill she would die on. This was her moment. She believed that there was something wrong at that farm, something that was going to happen tomorrow. She had tried every way she knew how to find out what it was, and this was her only option.

She drove her little car on the well travelled pathway, past Hopwoods and along to Northfield.

The little copse of trees on the corner was the place she had thought of to hide her car. There was a fair bit of scrub, it would keep the car from being obvious. Oh how she wished she had a four wheel drive, or at least a car that looked a bit more like every other car in the country. Her car stood out like a sore thumb. A bright yellow, sporty hatchback. What a stupid car to drive in the country. But she hid it as well as she could. She could walk the few hundred metres from the trees to the farm and then up the long, curved driveway. She was thankful for the lack of maintenance now, all the weeds and the scrub would give her places to hide on what would feel like a long walk up to the farm and back.

She stepped out of the car, pulled her hood forward over her face, and waited for her eyes to adjust to the dark. She wanted to use her torch as little as possible.

Then she started creeping up the highway towards the farm, ready to jump off the road at the least sound of a car.

But there was nothing. It was 2 a.m. and the roads were empty. More empty than she could have believed if she hadn't just lived in the country for a few months. How was it possible that everyone slept at night here? They woke at 4 a.m., sure, to milk cows and get started on the day, but there was just so little night-time activity.

The night was clear, there were so many stars in the sky. More stars than she had ever seen in her life. The sight made her feel small and insignificant, and at the very same time, connected and part of the universe. She understood now the great philosophers of the past. If they had spent any time looking up at this number of stars it would have made them think incredibly large thoughts. And so they had. She'd have to go looking in the library for more old books to see what this night sky did to a person.

She picked her way carefully across the cattle grid at the farm gate. This was no time to turn an ankle. She wished she could walk as quietly as they did in fantasy novels. You know, 'the Hobbit walked silently up the side of the hill through the bracken, not breaking a twig'? It would be lovely to be able to do that. Every step she took that led her closer to the farm house sounded louder and louder until each one sounded like an earthquake in her ears.

A thumping sound made her heart leap into her mouth and she froze until she realised it must just be a wallaby making its way through the bush. There was no other sound.

At the top of the driveway she turned left and with the darkened house behind her, made her quiet and cautious way to the new shed. Nothing was happening here. There was no light leaking out of the garage door. Everything was in darkness and silence. She was alone, as she had hoped.

She could hardly see anything but didn't dare to turn her torch on. She started to doubt herself. What had she hoped to find in this little excursion? She couldn't figure out if it was more scary when Angus was around, or in the dark like this when she was alone.

Well, she could go into the shed at least. Satisfy her curiosity. She had wanted to see what this brand new and shiny building housed since she first set foot on this farm on that very first day. And now she was sure that if she could have a quick look around she could figure out what was going on. If she didn't catch Angus doing something wrong, at least she might have some understanding of how he had brought the farm out of bankruptcy, what he was doing that had worked so well. All her work listening to the other farmers, getting to know their farms and their equipment, would come in handy. She could at least have a look in the shed and see what Angus was doing, and what equipment he had.

The shed rose up against the sky like a castle. She wondered if it was defended by a dragon, or as was more likely, by a noisy alarm. She looked around for places that she could hide if some alarm should sound. There. Over there was the hedge of the little kitchen garden. If she could make it to that, she could probably hide behind the hedge all the way back to the road, force her way somehow through the fence, and … she just hoped she wouldn't have to do it.

The big garage door at the front of the shed was obviously a no-go. It would be far too noisy to open. But there had to be a smaller door somewhere on the side. And no-one locked their doors here in the country, did they? That's what she was counting on.

She felt her way around the side of the shed. The shadows seemed to deepen here. Was it the evil in the farm? Was she totally being fanciful now? A torch would be handy but even at the back of the shed she felt too close to the house to try it. She just had to keep feeling. And then there was a door handle under her shaking fingers. She tried it. It turned.

This was it. This was really the point of no return. Once she got in, she would be breaking and entering, whatever she found. She could just give up now, and head back to her car. She could tell herself how brave she had been but how she wasn't going to be foolhardy. She could read the spreadsheets from Slimy Tom (how dare he read her private email over Evie's shoulder!) and tell herself that everything was OK.

But it wasn't OK. Something was going on here.

She turned the handle and walked into the shed.

Closing the door carefully behind her, she finally switched on her torch.

This was no vegetable packing shed. This was like no shed she had visited in the whole district. There was a lot of shiny metal equipment. Like oversized chemical reactors. There were big vats, and big drying belts. Lots of heating equipment. It looked … yep. Definitely suspicious. No wonder Angus was trying to keep people out.

Mel couldn't get much of a view with her tiny torch. There were no stars to help her see in here. But as the torch flashed around the shed the shine of metal came back to her.

And then, near the front doors, a different kind of shine like something was wrapped in plastic.

What was that?

Mel picked her way carefully to the front of the shed. She nearly tripped over cords lying in her way and at one point she kicked a bucket. The clang rang out loudly and she held her breath for what felt like a full five minutes before she moved forwards again with even more care.

There were pallets at the front, all ready for loading onto the trucks. But these pallets were not potatoes. What were they?

Little bricks of stuff wrapped securely in plastic. All the same size, all the same shape. They looked like play doh. Like clay. They looked like something out of that border protection TV program. That's what they looked like—drugs.

Mel pulled out her pocket knife. She cut into a corner of one of the bricks. It took forever, cutting through all the plastic that had been carefully wrapped around this thing. If Angus had taken as much care with his farm as he had with wrapping whatever this was, perhaps he wouldn't have had to do anything dodgy. But eventually she ripped some plastic off and dug out a bit of the white powder inside.

She was so tempted to touch it to her tongue, to see if she could figure out what it was. But she had no experience with drugs so it could have tasted like strawberries for all she knew. And she didn't want to lose her head.

Instead, Mel wrapped the little plug of stuff in the plastic and stuck it in her pocket. Tomorrow that would go straight to the police and she'd know for sure what the dodgy thing was that was going on in this place. But right now she had to get out of here.

And quickly.

She realised that she'd been hearing noises for a while. How long? She had no idea. She had been so involved in cutting through the plastic that she had lost track of all time, and now she could hear a truck and some voices.

Pieces fell into place in her mind. It was Friday, very early Friday but it was definitely Friday, and things were happening. Angus was doing what he had planned that night in the pub.

And then she felt a surge of panic. There was nowhere to hide in this shiny metal shed. She had to get out of here.

She dodged buckets and cords and serious equipment, praying that they would open the garage doors and that she could sneak out the side way. The talking sounded even clearer now. This was not good.

Mel stood just for an instant, her ear to the shed door, listening for voices outside. Listening for footsteps. But the sounds were coming from the front of the shed. There was nothing she could hear here at the side. Should she go out or not?

Then the choice was taken out of her hands, the garage door started to creak upwards, and Mel took a deep breath, opened the side door, and ducked outside.

There was no one there. They were all out the front.

She kept going, hood over face, ducking low, and made her way to the hedge on the kitchen garden.

She was breathing hard. Terrified. Half of her wanted to head straight to the car while the men here were occupied. But then she wouldn't know the whole story. She forced herself to stay and watch, using the overgrown kitchen garden to give her some cover, and her phone to video as much as could be possibly seen now that the shed lights were turned on.

The truck backed up to the shed had a familiar logo on the side. Thompson's. It was a company truck. She was indignant. How dare they? But what else did she expect?

There were four men working. Three from the farm and the truck driver. Angus, his silhouette unmistakeable, was in charge. The forklift was used to lift the pallets of the white stuff and stack them into the truck. Mel watched and waited while it happened.

Once the pallets were put in the men picked up some long strips of something—was it tin or wood, maybe? From the side of the shed. And they manoeuvred those into the truck too.

The driver closed the truck doors and Angus slapped him on the back and shook his hand. And the driver got into the cab of the truck and drove off the property.

Whatever their little operation was, it was over for now. Angus and the two others wandered back into the shed, presumably to tidy up and turn the lights off.

Mel stayed where she was, under the cover of the messy hedge. She wondered where the white powder came from and how it got into the shed in the first place. She felt in her pocket to make sure she still had her little sample. Good thing that they hadn't noticed the corner missing from one of the bricks.

And then she felt her pocket again. There was something missing. She'd left her knife in the shed. She'd put it down while she was wrapping the powder up, and she hadn't picked it up again.

And there was Angus, looking at something in his hand, then looking around to see where it came from.

She had to get out of there.

Now, what was the plan? Follow this hedge down to the fence, force your way through, or under, or over the fence somehow and get back to the car.

Her legs felt like blocks of concrete. Icy blocks of concrete. She'd been crouching in a stupid position for a while and she had no feeling in her feet. But she stumbled and skittered her way behind the hedge, not stopping to see if Angus was coming after her. She just had to get off the farm.

She pulled the wire of the fence down in a panic and managed to slide herself between that and the barbed wire on the top. She heard a bit of a tear but that was OK, she didn't intend to ever wear this jumper again. She would burn it as soon as possible.

She could hear Angus yelling at the Swanson boys. Were they looking for her? The shed door was closing. Maybe they were more interested in covering their own tracks than in looking for possible intruders. She had to hope so anyway.

She dodged her way to the car, sneaking between any bits of cover she could find. The sky was becoming lighter as dawn got closer and she didn't need to use her torch anymore.

She made it to the car without seeing anyone. Had it all worked? She was safe, wasn't she? She was in the car now. No-one chasing her could get in to the car to hurt her. She could get away.

Then she realised one drawback of her hidey hole. She would have to drive past the farm to get back to her house. There was no getting around it. It was a disaster. Why hadn't she thought this through? Surely there was another place she could have hidden that didn't require her to drive back past the farm. She felt like an idiot.

Ah well, there was no reason why she should be going for a nice drive … in the country … at five in the morning …

She's just have to take her chances. Or head out bush and then come back at ten or something. No. She pulled out of her hiding place and set her nose back to town. There was no point in trying to sneak past the farm, car engines make noise and she couldn't roll along a flat road.

She couldn't help looking up at the farm shed as she drove past. Was that Angus there looking at her? She couldn't tell. She shivered. She needed to see the police as soon as possible. That's all there was to it. Once she'd done that, she'd be safe.

She turned the heater up high and began to warm up. And began to relax. She'd done it! She'd been in that shed, seen what was going on, and no one had caught her, and she had evidence of the biggest crime she could imagine.

She was right. There was something dodgy about that farm. And she could prove it. And everyone would know that she was right.

She laughed in relief, she was giddy with relief. Ecstatic.

Wait until she told Evie.

She was going to have a nap, a coffee, and then straight to the police.

15

Mel fell into a deep sleep and woke at about 10 a.m. shaking in fear from a nightmare where Angus stalked her through the bush and behind trees. How could she have slept at all? She should have just stayed awake and gone to the police. Or even headed to their house and woken them up. But where was Graham's house? She had no idea.

As she showered and dressed she berated herself for not finding these important things out sooner. If you're thinking you'll uncover a crime, knowing who to report it to would be one of the first things to work out, you'd think. Yet Mel had left out this important step in her planning.

Still, she was here, her house was secure, the locks showed no sign of being played with. Maybe she was over reacting. Maybe Angus hadn't found her knife, hadn't been worried about it. Maybe she had got away with it completely.

Once she got to the coffee though, she thought again. Maybe Angus couldn't come looking for her because he had to be at the farm to load the produce into the truck. The legal produce. Maybe he was biding his time. How long did it take to load vegetables?

She looked at the sample she had taken last night. This was her triumph but it was a pretty sad and messy looking sample. Some triumph. She had the video too. She had a look at her phone, playing it back. Dark shadows doing shadowy things. Would Graham even take her seriously?

She had to try.

She put on her coat and walked into town and up to the police station, fingering the little parcel in her pocket all the way. Lost in her thoughts she pushed on the door, and came up short. She tried the handle again and found that it was locked.

Looking up she saw a sign posted in the window beside the door stating that Senior Constable Graham Scott was over at Ellenworth for the day, and for urgent enquiries she should ring 000 or Crime Stoppers. That's what Angus had said in the pub—Graham and Ellenworth. Graham was away. It was all planned.

Mel stopped. Her tired brain didn't know what to do. She took the next logical step and went to the café to drink coffee and try to think it through.

Was this urgent? Should she ring 000? She would really like to talk to an actual police officer and someone who knew the town. She wanted to get someone else's take on what was going on. Now that she was sitting in comfort in the broad light of day, what she had seen in the shed took on a sense of unreality and she just wasn't so sure of herself anymore.

She had no way of knowing what was in the little parcel she had in her pocket. She wanted to be sure. What if she was wrong? What if there was another, perfectly sensible explanation?

The stuff in the packets was, say, salt, or sugar. And the farm was hiding them in the truck because they wanted cheap transport of this good, and were just ripping off the company for transport costs, not because they had illegal drugs.

She could probably test that theory by tasting the stuff she held in her pocket. But she didn't want to do that.

She just wasn't sure.

She lifted her coffee mug to her lips for one last sip and realised that she'd finished the whole drink. In the end, she decided to leave the reporting until Graham came back. The drugs (or whatever it was) had left the farm now anyway. The evidence would stay the same for another day. She would just go into her office and work.

That would be safer anyway. What if Angus saw her hanging around the police station or caught word that she was turning him in. What if Crime Stoppers or 000 didn't take her seriously? What if they told her not to worry about it? Then she'd be in the poo without any help at all. No, it would be better to wait until Graham came back and hand it all over to him.

At the office she tried to work but the normal daily activities didn't hold sway. She was so tired. And she was so worried. She took the little parcel out of her pocket and stared at it again. This was the only evidence she had. It had to stay safe.

The only lockable thing in her office was the filing cabinet. She put the parcel in an envelope and labelled it 'For the police'. Then she locked it in the bottom drawer of the filing cabinet, at the back underneath the files.

But somehow it wasn't enough. She had thought she could get through this on her own, that she could be in control. Now that she was alone, she finally realised how much she needed others. Jason wasn't here to help. Graham was away. Emma? No she couldn't dump this on Emma, and she didn't even know whether she could trust anyone in the town. Who was involved besides Angus and his thugs? She had no idea.

But there was one person she could trust. She just hoped she'd answer the phone.

And this time, things went right, and she did.

'Mel! So nice to hear from you!'

'Evie, are we alone?'

'What? I'm just in the office here. No problem, we can chat.'

'Evie, listen to me, I'm serious here, is ... you know who ... there with you in the office.'

'Who Tom? Yes, he's here. Why? Why are you being so strange.'

Mel cursed. So much for keeping this call a secret. Tom could probably hear every word she was saying. If he wasn't suspicious, he would be now. She had to think quickly.

'I just need someone to whinge to, you know, about ... girly stuff. And I don't really want him to hear me. Do you think you could take a five minute break and head out to the hallway or something?'

'Girly stuff? Mel you're so funny.' Evie giggled like some blonde valley girl. 'OK, hang on then. But if Tom docks my hours, I'm coming to you for the money.'

'It'll only be five minutes. There's just no-one I can talk to here like I talk to you.' Mel was nearly making herself sick with the pretence. She hoped Evie could switch into serious mode when she needed her to.

'OK, just hang on,' said Evie. Mel heard a rustle as she got up, then the sounds of chatter and background office work were suddenly muted.

'OK, I'm in the breakout room now. Mel, what is this about?' Evie asked in a much calmer and more serious voice.

'I knew you couldn't be as giggly as you sounded.'

'I'm trying to make a good impression on Tom.'

Mel winced.

'Are you sure that's the best way to go about it?'

How would women's equality get off the ground if everyone turned into a Marilyn Monroe sound-alike when flirting?

'Anyway, I don't think you'll want to be his best mate soon. Evie, I went to Northfield last night, well, more of early this morning really. And I saw what I thought was drugs there. Like, some white powder in those bricks, like you see on the TV.'

'What? Mel, are you having me on?'

'I'm completely serious.' Mel told Evie about her adventure and the more she talked the more surreal it sounded.

'Anyway, that's what I saw. And the drug sample, or whatever it is, it's locked in the bottom drawer of my filing cabinet.'

'Mel, that's a really serious accusation.'

'I know it is. So I need your help. I'm going to go to the police here but I need you to look into things on your end.'

'Oh, I don't know if I should get involved.' Evie sounded more than unsure, she sounded downright determined to say no.

'It's just that things can't just be happening from this end. Someone needs to be looking after the … the … whatever I found at the delivery end too. This is really serious.'

'You're telling me.'

'I'm not making things up. I was risking my life last night. I'm not asking you to do anything like that.'

'Mmmmm …'

'Evie, how long have we been friends?'

Eventually Evie gave in. 'OK Mel, what do you want me to do.'

'I need you to get into Tom's computer.'

'Hang on, you're not blaming Tom for this? I know you hate him, but this is crazy.'

'No. No, he could just be an innocent … they could just be using him too.' Mel cursed to herself, why did Evie have to be so smitten with that smarmy guy? Should she have tried to get someone else onside? But there wasn't anyone else to ask. 'You told me that all the Northfield data was on Tom's computer. Now, Angus could be hiding the trail well, but now we know what to look for, I'm sure you can find something in the records. But we need to get hold of them off Tom's computer. We need to know who the truck driver is. We need to know all the details of all deliveries to and from Northfield. It's important.'

There was silence on the other end of the phone. Mel was asking a lot, and she knew it. But there was no one else to turn to.

And Mel was very sure that Tom was involved. Jason had told her that Angus had left school in grade nine to work on the farm. Manipulating the documents to hide the extra profit was surely beyond a thug like him. But Evie would have to find that out herself. Mel hoped that her infatuation wouldn't blind her.

Mel heard a huge sigh from the other end of the phone.

'OK, I'll do it. Or I'll try. You want me to get the Northfield data. How the hell am I going to do that? I've been trying, but Tom won't give me anything and he's beginning to wonder why I'm asking all the time. That's why I keep putting you off.'

'How? You've been watching Tom's every move for the last three months. You know his password, I'm sure of it. You knew mine and I never showed you, and you were never as interested in me as you have been in Tom.'

'Look, I know you don't like Tom, I know you think he's been after your job. But he's not to blame for the inaccuracies of the reporting from the Tasmanian region. We've talked a bit about the level four promotion and he thinks that's what's standing in your way. And he's said that he's sorry it happened to you, that it could happen to anyone. He's such a nice guy. I think you've got him all wrong. Look at all the gifts he's given me. He gave me the most beautiful painting of a lily, I have it on my desk. Look at all the times we've gone out. I thought …'

'Hang on. I'm not to blame either. Why are you talking about my mistakes? You remember that the level four promotion was the cover story for why I'm out here? You're not believing your own propaganda are you?' Evie was supposed to be spreading these stories to get rid of suspicion, not to trick herself into believing them.

'No, no. He was talking to me. He was saying how he knew I was missing you and that I couldn't blame you for little mistakes like that.'

Mel smiled grimly. It was so good of Slimy Tom to stand up for her. Not. She could see his agenda to drive the two friends apart even if Evie couldn't.

'Evie, have I ever led you wrong on a guy?'

Evie was quiet for a long time. Mel wondered if she'd pushed it too far. 'Are you OK Evie?'

'You're right. You've never led me wrong. It's just that I really thought that this was the guy. The guy for me. I was hoping …'

'He hasn't asked you to move in with him has he?'

'He was hinting about it yesterday.'

'I'm really sorry, truly I am. And he might be totally clean. And if he is, I promise you, you have my blessing. I'll take back everything I've ever said. I won't call him Slimy Tom ever again. But surely it's better to find out now than to get locked in with a criminal for life.'

'But not trusting him. That's not a good start to a relationship.'

'But being married to a drug dealer, that's not a good ending.'

'Mmm …' said Evie.

Mel put her head in her free hand. This was so hard. Why couldn't Evie trust her?

'Look, it's not you that's not trusting him. It's me. It's me calling on our long friendship to find out what's happening at Northfield. It's me needing you to get me information so that I can do my job well. However you want to phrase it, put the blame on me. I'm the one needing you to do this snooping. Will you do it for me?'

There was another silence, so long that Mel rose from her chair and paced around the room. But in the end Evie came through.

'OK, I'll find everything I can about Northfield in his files. He has a management meeting with Sharon this afternoon. I'll have a fairly free hand then. I'll do my best Mel, but I really hope you're wrong.'

'Evie, you're a darling. You're a wonderful friend. You are my confidant. I knew I could depend on you.'

'Don't push it. I really don't want to do this. I'd better go, Tom's looking at me through the window. What am I going to tell him we

145

talked about?'

'Tell him anything you like. Tell him I've fallen in love and that I'm trying to make a decision about staying here in the country.'

'Oooo Mel? Have you fallen in love?' Suddenly the brainless giggle was back.

'Evie, get back to work. Let me know as soon as you find out anything.'

Mel hung up and sighed. That was harder than she thought it would be. Why did the silly girl have to go and fall for someone as obviously fake and slimy as Tom?

16

As the day wore on, Mel's sense of unease grew. The thought of spending the night alone started to scare her. What if Angus was just waiting until the evening to find her and ...

She ran through her options.

She could spend the night in the office. No, first that would be uncomfortable, and secondly it would be just as unsafe as the house. And this old place probably was full of creaks and groans like her house was but she didn't know the creaks and groans of this place and she wouldn't be able to relax at all.

She could go and stay with Emma or Merryn. But then she would be putting them in danger. Nope, she wasn't going to put anyone in danger if she could help it.

But she didn't want to stay alone at home either.

Should she just drive out to Ellenworth and find Graham? Or camp out at the front of his house until he came home?

She was just overreacting, she thought. No one had seen her. And who is to say that even if they had seen her they would be violent?

But the thought of the thugs she had seen loading the truck dogged her through the day. Whether they were coming for her or not, she was scared.

What was she going to do?

At the end of the day she was no closer to a conclusion. She locked her office door and crept slowly down the stairs. As she opened the building door to go out on the street she was on edge, looking for Angus's thugs around every corner.

She walked up the street and heard fast footsteps behind her. She turned, ready to scream blue murder, and saw Jason. At first she was relieved, but then her suspicions rose again.

Why was he here? Was he in on it too? Was he checking in on her for Angus? Was the enmity between the two farm managers just a big ruse?

'Hello,' she said, a little breathless, trying to act normal.

'Hey.' Jason looked amazing, real and solid, comforting. It was all she could do to not throw herself into his arms and tell him everything. But she held back. She didn't know who to trust.

'Are you OK?' he asked. 'You don't look too well.'

The two of them walked on together.

'Yeah, I'm feeling a little under the weather.' Mel thought that was a reasonable thing to say. 'I think I might be coming down with something. I'm just not sleeping well. I've been feeling a bit edgy, you know? In that house by myself. It's scary here at night.'

Oh no, that sounded like she wanted him to stay over. And to be honest, she did.

'I know what you're saying. I like having Bella around, she's company when I'm blue.'

Now that was an idea. Bella could stay with her, just for the night. She would scare off any intruders.

'Do you think maybe you could share her with me? Just for a night.'

'You want Bella?' Jason stopped and stared at her. 'You. Want Bella to stay the night?'

Mel cursed her harsh words about the dog. She wished she could eat them all now.

'Well, you keep telling me what a well-behaved dog she is. And she wags her tail when she sees me now. I think I could give it a go. If I like having her there, I might just get my own dog.'

Mel walked on, not looking Jason in the eye, hoping she sounded reasonable.

Jason was shaking his head as they walked along. Then he touched her arm and turned her to look at him.

'Are you sure you're OK? There's nothing else going on here?'

Mel looked at his sympathetic eyes. Either he was an amazing actor, or he knew nothing about what Northfield was doing, and her place in the whole story. But still, it was a risk.

She shook her head. 'It's complicated. I can't … Look, can you lend me Bella? Just for tonight? Do you think she'd come?'

'Sure, she'd come. Especially if you give her treats. I can give you a bag of them. If that's what you need.'

As they walked up to the front door of the blue weatherboard house Jason invited her in for dinner.

'It won't be anything special but I'm happy to share. And you can spend a little time with Bella here and make sure you're OK with this.' Jason still couldn't believe what she was asking, Mel could tell. And she really didn't want to go back to her own home. So she accepted.

The house felt comfortable and cosy. Not what Mel expected from a bachelor pad. She wondered how much influence Dot had on the interior decoration. The colour scheme was black and maroon. There was a Turkish rug on the polished floorboards, a small lounge suite and some beautiful polished wood coffee tables that she later learned were made by Frank as a house-warming present.

She sat on the couch and patted the dog while Jason prepared a cup of tea. Bella was happy for the attention, laying her head on Mel's knee. No treats were needed, the big black scary dog was now a friendly ball of softness.

Mel rubbed the dog's belly and wondered whether she was going to be enough of a protection through the night. But then she remembered the horrific barking when Bella had something to protect. The barking that had greeted her on that early morning jog. Bella would be a good guard dog tonight. If there was anything to be guarded from.

Drink finished and dog placated, Mel joined Jason in the kitchen. In no time she was chatting freely with him, helping him to chop up vegetables for an aromatic soup.

'You know, I didn't even like cooking before I came out here.' Mel took the green beans and started to top and tail them. 'But now, I guess there aren't so many other options here or something. But I'm really enjoying the creativity of it.'

'I know. At uni there were so many different kinds of take away food available—Indian one night, Thai the next. I just didn't bother with it.'

'Did you cook as a child?'

'Mum's a bit of a genius in the kitchen. Sometime you're going to have to try her scones. She takes them to the farmer's market. So I picked up a few things here and there. Of course, I add some very different flavours. Her curry was dead boring. She needed to learn a bit from me when I got back.'

'Oh, that reminds me. How was the dinner last night? I didn't expect you back here so soon.'

'It was great, really. Mum and Dad are still down there for the weekend but, I guess—well I thought about what you were saying. I thought someone should be around to check that the farm is OK. I made some sort of excuse for Mum and Dad and came back.'

Mel swallowed and wondered if she should say more about her adventures. Jason seemed to be finally trusting her only now it was too late. Why hadn't he been a bit more trusting? Why couldn't he have come with her to Northfield? She didn't want to drag him into her mess now. Dragging the dog in was probably enough.

'Is the farm OK?' she asked.

'Yeah, I went out this afternoon, everything is fine.'

'Well … good.'

The two of them kept working on the soup together. The comfortable silence continued for a while and was broken by Bella padding into the kitchen and pushing her head under Mel's hand for more pats. Mel laughed and Jason looked over and nodded.

'She's your best friend now,' he said. 'I think the sleepover will go well tonight.'

17

After a warming dinner of soup and crusty bread, Mel felt comfortable and happy and was sure that her fears were a figment of her imagination. But still, she was grateful for Jason's offer to walk her home, and for the promise of Bella's company.

Jason wished her a good night at the door, and Mel took the dog inside.

Bella immediately began checking the place out, sniffing every corner, checking out every room. It was like having a small child over, Mel thought, as she collapsed on the futon couch. She would just sit for a while and let Bella check everything over and then she would go to bed. She was so tired. It had been a long couple of days.

Mel didn't wake up when Bella jumped on the futon next to her and curled up to sleep by her side. But she did notice when Bella pricked her head up and started to growl softly a few hours later.

'What is it, girl?' She asked, and then she could hear the car slowly crawling by her house. And then the noise stopped and she was tempted to relax again, but Bella was at the door by this time, ears pricked and her whole body on alert.

Mel pulled herself off the couch and went to check that the door was locked. And then the whole world seemed to explode around her.

Bella went mad with barking. The door was bashed open (the lock didn't stand a chance) and the two men burst through. Bella threw herself at them and was knocked to the side by one of the thugs. She lay on the floor whimpering.

Mel was grabbed roughly and thrown onto the floor, a firm hand forced over her mouth to muffle her screams. She struggled, but the two men held her down and tied her hands and feet. She had no chance really. She was not strong enough to stand against this, and Bella, her one line of defence, had fallen at the first hurdle.

She knew she was going to die.

18

Mel was gagged, bundled roughly into a car, and driven out of the town. She had some idea of where she was going and she was right. The men, the Swanson boys, Angus's thugs, took her into the new and shiny shed and tied her to a chair.

Part of her wanted to laugh at how clichéd this was. How trite. Was Angus truly trying to recreate a movie?

Angus removed her gag and she tried to swallow. She could taste blood in her mouth. Her arms ached from being tied behind her and the muscles in her legs screamed, begging her to move them, but she couldn't.

The shed was brightly lit, tonight all the fluorescent lights were switched on. Mel could clearly see the reactors, filters and drying apparatus that she had picked out last night with her torch. (Was it just one night ago? It felt like weeks had passed since that foolish adventure.) It was clear that this setup had nothing to do with vegetables, and she could understand why Angus kept everyone away from his farm to avoid what could be costly glances through doors mistakenly left open.

She wondered whether Angus had thought this all through himself. The apparatus looked costly and complicated. How did he know what to do? Maybe he wasn't as dim as Jason thought he was. Maybe he had found that drug-making was worth the effort of learning a bit of science. Or maybe he had help. But who would have helped him?

'So she's awake. Let's see if she'll talk,' Angus growled and Mel realised that he was going to try to recreate every movie cliché that he could. She was torn between the temptation to join in with the movie quotes, or to laugh at him. Then she realised that neither option was good. This brute was determined to hurt her. Tears came to her eyes. She was no hero and she wished she could die simply now, that she could will herself to die, without going through any more pain.

But that wasn't going to be. Angus slapped her face just to let her know who was boss. Then he brought his horrible mouth so close that she gagged from the sour smell of his breath as he yelled at her. 'What did you see last night? And who did you tell?'

'How do you know I saw anything?' Mel asked.

He laughed grimly. 'You need to buy a less recognisable car if you want to get away with snooping around the farms.'

Mel cursed. So she had been seen. She couldn't get out of this. She couldn't pretend it wasn't her and it was stupid of her to think that she had got away with it.

'What did you see?' Angus yelled right in her face. Mel flinched, his breath smelled awful.

'Nothing. Just the truck,' she whimpered, then with more gusto: '*Our* truck.'

'So what if it was *your* truck,' Angus spat on the ground. 'Your truck trucks our goods. Nothing wrong with that.'

'If there's nothing wrong, why am I here?'

'You know why you're here. What did you see?'

Mel wondered what to say, what would make her look authentic but get her into the least amount of trouble. What could she say that would convince this oaf that she wasn't dangerous?

'I ... I saw you put something in the truck ... from this shed.'

'And?' Angus hit her again.

'And I guessed it was something ... dodgy, but I was ... I was behind the hedge. I couldn't see much at all.'

Mel flinched as his hand raised against her again. This guy was getting off on beating her up. She hoped he wouldn't give his thugs a go as well. She hoped she wouldn't die. She hoped ...

'You were in the shed.'

'No.' Mel shook her head. But Angus was having none of that. He brought out her pocket knife and waved it in her face.

'You shouldn't leave these presents behind if you don't want questions.'

Mel shook her head again, swallowing hard. But Angus didn't believe her and this punch took the breath from her lungs.

'Who did you tell?' Yes, that was the next obvious question.

'Nobody.' Smack.

'I swear, I told nobody. I was going to go straight to Graham but he's not in town and I was going to go tell him tomorrow.' Apparently this answer was more believable. Well, it was the truth.

'You didn't think this was important enough to tell anyone?'

'Well … I didn't really know what I'd seen,' said Mel. The image of the envelope locked in the bottom of the filing cabinet was filling her mind, she almost worried that Angus could see it by looking in her eyes. 'You're ripping off the company but it's not a grade-A crime.' Mel braced herself again for another punch. But if anything was going to convince Angus that she hadn't seen the drugs, this would. And then maybe, maybe he wouldn't kill her.

He would kill her though, she knew it. You can't just rough someone up and then send them back into the community with a 'be a good girl and don't tell anyone about this'.

Angus stepped back. He appeared to be thinking. Then he absent-mindedly smacked her again and signalling to his thugs to join him, he walked out of the shed.

What was he going to do? And why hadn't she told anyone in Lillyford what she'd seen? If she'd gone to see Graham she wouldn't be in this position now. If she'd just told Jason what she suspected, he would have had the sense to do something more than just leave her with the dog.

The poor dog.

Mel now wished Bella hadn't stayed over. She hadn't been the help that Mel had hoped for, though she had given it her all, and now all that had come of Mel's great idea was that a beautiful friendly dog had been hurt, had maybe lost her life, trying to save a stupid human.

Mel felt tears come to her eyes. How could she have been so stupid? And who would care if she died anyway? Evie would go on and marry Slimy Tom and be happy in the city. And her father would have the burden that she was taken off his hands. And no-one in this town would care, they'd only known her for the blink of an eye.

She sniffed loudly and realised that her attackers had left her alone for a minute. She could see them, just outside the door in the shadows. She could hear Angus grunting out orders. What were they planning to do now? Mel wanted to be able to think of a plan of escape. She looked around the brightly lit shed. Even if she could get out of this chair, where could she hide? There was no way she could outrun them. She couldn't think, couldn't find a way through, and as she realised there was no escape, the tears started coming. She didn't bother trying to stop them. Who would care that the snot was running out of her nose and that she couldn't wipe it away? Who would notice the running mascara that she hadn't even removed at the end of the day? Who cared? She was going to die anyway.

19

The sound of whimpering under his window woke Jason. He laughed to himself. It sounded like even though Mel was willing to spend the night with Bella, Bella wasn't so keen on returning the favour and had found a way to escape and come home. She was a smart dog.

He got up to let her in, not bothering to turn the lights on as she slunk through the door with her tail between her legs. Then she whined as he patted her and he felt something sticky and wet on his hands. He took her into the kitchen and turned the light on to see better.

He could see the damage to her face, the blood. What was going on?

He reached for his phone. He knew one person who wouldn't mind being woken in the middle of the night to care for a hurt animal.

'Emma? Look, I don't have time to explain but Bella's been hurt. Can you come to my place and look after her? I have to go.'

He pulled on some clothes and boots and walked out into the darkness. He needed to find out what had happened to Mel.

She had been scared last night, and he was pretty sure it wasn't Mel who had done this damage to the dog. There was something very wrong here that she hadn't seen fit to tell him about. He'd start at her house, he was pretty sure he wouldn't find her there, but it was the first place to go.

He stepped through Mel's open door, noticing the way the doorframe had been splintered, his fears grew and he reached for his phone again to call Graham.

'Hello?' came the sleepy mumble.

'Graham you need to come to Mel's place on View St. There's

something you need to see.'

'Be right there.'

Jason pulled his sleeve over his hand and turned the lights on. He crept around the room, checking out the damage. 'Mel?' He called hopefully, but he was pretty sure there'd be no answer.

He was heading up the hallway to make sure she wasn't hiding in the bedroom or something, when the theme from The Twilight Zone started playing. Was he imagining things? Was this all some kind of elaborate practical joke? Graham would kill him if he'd called him out of bed all for nothing.

Then he realised, it was Mel's phone ringing. What a crazy ring tone she had. It was one of the things he loved about her, her stupid sense of humour. So much like his. But it had really bitten him this time.

He grabbed her bag and answered the phone just before it rang out. But before he could say hello, a charming voice on the other end just started talking.

'Mel, you were right. I didn't think you'd answer, it's so late but I had to ring and tell you. I've spent all night working through the files on Northfield and it took some undoing, that's for sure. But Slimy Tom is slimy alright and there's something seriously wrong with these books. The numbers just don't add up. Or they add up to something they are not supposed to. How did you work it out? I mean, it's just crazy. They must be running drugs or something. The product volumes are all out of whack. I reckon they're using a false floor or a false wall or something in the trucks and then just putting the veg in on top. And you know that truck that lost its goods that you got in trouble for? That was one of Tom's trucks, not yours. He did the swap on the books. I guess his false floor malfunctioned or something but it's all here.' Eventually the voice ran down. 'Mel?'

Jason paused. He didn't know what to say.

'Um …' he started.

'You're not Mel!'

'I'm Jason.'

'Oh, hi Jason, it's Evie. I've wanted to meet you. Mel tells me lots about you. Look I really need to talk to Mel, is she there?'

Jason smiled at that, it was nice to know that Mel thought about him.

Then he looked around at the damage in the room and fear gripped him.

Evie repeated herself, 'Is Mel there? I've really got to talk with her.'

'She's not here. I'm at her house and it's ... Look, can you tell me again, from the beginning, what you've found out about Northfield? I'm at Mel's place and it's been broken into. I'm waiting for the police. If you can tell me what's going on, I'm sure it will help.'

Evie started again, telling a much more measured story, and when Graham walked through the door, his eyes widening as he took in the scene, Jason put the phone on to speaker and they sat at the kitchen table listening to the her tale.

Once Evie had told all she knew, Graham spoke.

'I'm going to ring your local police, and tell them to contact you. You need forensic IT to come and check over those files and to collect Tom's computer from work. You must not open your door to anyone who isn't police, do you understand?'

Evie understood and Jason hung up the phone and looked at Graham.

'Where do we go from here?'

'Unless you can think of any special place Angus uses, we'll start at the farm and move on from there. You can drive, I'll make phone calls on the way.'

'Right!' Jason agreed and pulling the door closed behind them, they set off.

20

Mel felt better after a good cry. Cleansed, even. Able to think a bit more clearly.

In fact, after the cry was over all she really wanted was a free hand and a tissue just so she could blow her nose and have it all finished with. But that wasn't going to happen.

She struggled a bit but she was very securely tied up. She thought about the movies she watched. Perhaps if she could edge the chair closer to some equipment, she could rub her bonds against a sharp piece of metal or something. Or she could ...

Or, of course, she could fall over and be in a worse position than she was to start with. And who knew how Angus would react to her trying to escape. The guy was insane. No ... actually he wasn't insane. He was scarily, eerily sane. He was a bully. He was trying to protect his investment, his property, his income.

He walked back into the shed, brandishing his phone at her. So that's what he'd been doing, talking with his boss. Whoever that was.

'It's your lucky day, bitch,' he said. 'Tom here, says I should let you go. He says you're smart enough to know that you'll die if you tell on us. And that he can pin the blame on you anyway. He says he's done it before, and he'll do it again.'

'What?'

Mel heard squawking coming from the phone, and Angus put it on speaker.

'What we're going to do,' Mel heard the oily tones of Slimy Tom, 'is give you a nice injection, it will make you feel great. Then we'll send you home. If any of this comes to light we'll tell people you're a user. You will be too, we'll make sure of that. And we'll blame the whole thing on you. Obviously you're the mastermind of the operation, that's why you gave in so easily to Sharon and moved out there.'

It was Tom, Slimy Tom, more slimy than she had even imagined. And smart too. Her stomach clenched and she felt unable to breathe. Any hope she'd had of escaping due to Angus's lack of intelligence disappeared.

'But I tell you, I don't know what you're doing. I saw nearly nothing.' It was worth a try but she didn't really have any hope of convincing Tom of her innocence.

'You saw enough. You're a smart girl, Mel. You've been poking around ever since you got to that hole of a town. You know we're making heroin. I'm not stupid. I'm just going to make sure you never tell anyone else.'

'It won't work,' Mel whispered.

'Oh it will. You'll make it work. Because if you tell anyone what's going on, be sure that we'll take you down.'

'You can't …'

'You know I can. It's easy to shift the blame around if you know the software. So you're going to be quiet.'

Mel rallied herself. 'How do I explain my house? Angus's thugs did a lot of damage there.'

'I'm sure you'll come up with a convincing story. It's either that, or dying now. Which would you prefer?'

Mel hung her head and Angus cackled.

'I think we're good, Tom.'

'Good,' came the grunt from the phone.

Then, as Angus hung up, there came another, 'Good.' Followed swiftly by, 'Angus Harmley, you're under arrest.'

Angus swung around, fist outstretched to slam whoever was talking to him, then he saw Graham with his right hand on his holster, ready for action, and he froze.

'Smart move,' said Jason, and he handcuffed Angus as Graham finished the arrest spiel. 'And we'll have to thank your mate Tom for his highly incriminating words later.'

'Jason. The thugs …' said Mel.

'What thugs?'

'There were two thugs that came and picked me up. If they are around …'

Graham paused on his way out the door. 'There's no-one outside. Looks like Gus here sent them home. Did you Gus?'

Angus looked sly. 'They're here. They're just up … up in the field. I just need to call them and we'll outnumber you and you'll be—'

'Nah, I'd say they're gone,' said Graham. 'But you go ahead and yell if you want to.'

Angus's shoulders slumped.

'Didn't need 'em. They done what I wanted. And I need them tomorrow early for loading.'

'Well, that's not going to happen is it? Sounds like it's just the Swanson boys that you get to do your dirty work for you. They work on the farm, and they work on the side to do your extra jobs. Is that right?'

'Not sayin'.' Angus sounded surly and defeated.

'I'll go and pick them up then. I'm sure Mel here will recognise them.' Graham moved down to the garage door and pressed the open switch. 'Jason, you stay here with Mel until the ambulance comes. I'll radio for it as soon as I get in my car. I'm taking Angus to the cells and then I'll go on to the Swansons'. Everyone good with that?'

Jason was busy cutting through the tape that held Mel to the chair but Mel nodded. Angus cursed and swore but Graham told him that no-one was interested in his opinion and they ducked under the slowly opening door and disappeared into the night.

This time, once she was free, Mel didn't hold back from falling into Jason's arms and crying on his shoulder. She felt it was warranted. And he didn't seem to mind.

21

Mel sat at her computer in her little office, staring out the window to the river, trying to figure out how to phrase her final report without the whole thing sounding like a pulp-fiction novel. But that was hard with a story like this one.

Northfield had been going bankrupt, just like Jason said, and Slimy Tom was well aware of the fact, having done the spreadsheets for Northfield for years. Tom saw his opportunity and approached Angus with a money-making project. Mel wondered how long it had taken to get the idea through to Angus' brain.

Poppies grow well in northern Tasmania, there's a well-established industry making opioids for big pharmaceutical companies. But the poppies that Angus grew were slightly different, bred for high morphine content that could easily be turned to heroin. Tom gave Angus strict instructions on the heroin-making process and helped him to buy the equipment and set up the shed.

Then it was just a case of setting up a false wall in the back of the refrigerated trucks, loading the pallets of heroin in, and covering them up with the thin layer of sheeting that Mel had seen as she crouched in the kitchen garden. The truck driver was in on it, of course.

The false wall affected the count of vegetables loaded into the heroin-trafficking truck, which led to the anomalies that Mr Thompson had been worried about. There were other outcomes too, from the trafficking. Sometimes loads were delayed in order to avoid police investigations, sometimes they went off-track in order to deliver the goods to the dealers.

Slimy Tom worked his magic on the spreadsheets but even he wasn't able to hide all of the inconsistencies.

Then Mel came in and stuck her nose in where it wasn't wanted. And uncovered the whole thing.

She'd already given a statement to Graham, and she was aware she'd be used as a witness for the court case. She was being treated as a bit of a hero right now in the town, the farmers were happy that they would now be paid for full loads and no one was too concerned about Angus getting what he deserved. But she didn't feel great about being a hero. She was ready to hang up her super-suit and do some much more mundane work, like implementing the energy efficiency changes in the farms that were her cover story. She wanted the best for this little community now. She'd grown quite attached to it.

Mel saw Evie picking her way up the gravel garden path in four-inch heels. This was a party, she should have known that Evie would be determined to wear party clothes no matter how difficult it would make it to walk here. Mel was excited to have Evie here in what she now thought of as her new home. She had convinced Evie to stay a week and she was excited to put her futon to good use now that her front door had been fixed. She was using all of the spare rooms in her house, actually. Her father had come for the party as well. Mel wasn't sure if he was happy to have her safe, or feeling guilty that she was put in so much danger. But he was more attentive to her now than he'd been in quite a few years.

It had been four weeks since that adventurous night. Mel had taken some time to heal, and time to let the dust settle. But she wanted a party to say thank you to those who had saved her life.

Jason hadn't been so thrilled about the party. He didn't want attention directed at him. He didn't feel like he'd done enough.

'I should have stayed with you the whole night. I knew you were worried about something. I wish you could have trusted me.'

'I just didn't know. I mean, your dislike of Angus could have been a very clever ruse. I was so sure that he couldn't be running any clandestine operation on his own—there had to be some brains behind it.'

'Yes, but the brains were Slimy Tom's, not mine.'

'How was I supposed to know?'

'I hope you can trust me now.'

That was answered with more than just words. After the first falling into Jason's arms that night, Mel had found herself falling with more regularity. And enjoying it. And Dot and Frank were quite happy with that situation too.

In the end Mel and Jason decided that the party could be in honour of Bella. It was Bella who had really saved the day.

The door was wide open and Mel rushed out and gave Evie a hug.

'Welcome! So good to see you.'

'I've brought you a housewarming gift. I don't know how far you're going with decorating your house, but I don't want this anymore.'

'Is this the lily painting that Tom gave you? I'm not sure whether to say thanks or not.'

'Every time you look at it you can think of your major triumph.'

'Oh boy, I don't really ever want to think of that time again. It was …'

'If you don't like it, you can throw it. Seriously. And I have another gift for you in the car.'

'It is a lovely painting though, isn't it? I wonder whether I could hang it over the fireplace?'

'I'm sure your handyman boyfriend will show you how. Which one is he?' Evie's voice dropped to a whisper as they moved into the lounge room.

'He's over there, on the couch, chatting with my father. They have been in each other's pockets since Father got here. They get along really well, apparently.'

'Well that's something that has never happened with one of your boyfriends before.'

'It's something that I've never tried, to be honest. But hey, it's working so far. Father has all sorts of plans for Hopwoods. But Jason's holding his own.'

'And where's the guest of honour?'

'I reckon she's in the kitchen. Come and meet Emma and Merryn. They are putting the finishing touches on lunch and if I know anything about them, Bella is getting fed all the treats and scraps. But it's her party, so we'll let her get away with it. Oh, and while you're here you can talk with Emma about Melbourne. She's heading over there to start uni next year.'

'How did you convince her to do that?'

'Jason told her that if she was happy to be woken in the middle of the night to care for Bella, then maybe it was her duty to get the training to do it properly and to help all the animals in need. And I told her that if I could be brave enough to risk going to Northfield in the middle of the night, she could be brave enough to go to uni. She seemed to believe us.'

Leaving Evie in the kitchen with the exotically dressed Merryn (who was wearing a specially knitted celebration hat covered in poppies) and the now brave Emma, Mel headed back to the front door. There were some very special guests coming and they were running a little bit late.

Ah, here they were now. Dot and Frank, and in the back seat of their sedan a beautifully groomed and cheerful Bob and Alma.

'Oh good, you brought them!' Mel said to Dot as she helped them out of the car.

'It took a bit of doing. Alma's still not sure where she is or why.'

Bob unfolded himself slowly from the back of the car and offered his arm to Alma who grasped it like a lifeline.

'I guess it's you I have to thank for our new digs.'

'Are you liking the unit? I didn't really want to make you move, you know.' Mel hovered like a nervous mother hen as she walked slowly up the pathway slowly on the other side of Bob.

'I know, it was our stupid boy who brought it on himself. No one said he should do something illegal like that.'

'I'm sure he was trying to help.'

'Growing poppies and making heroin is a bloody stupid way to try to help. There's no getting around it,' Bob growled. 'But the new place is good. And the arthritis is a bit better with the right medicines. And young Jason is looking after the farm quite well.'

'Well, that's very good to hear. Now come in and have a seat and I'm sure Merryn will get you a nice drink of something.'

The house filled up with guests: Henry and Jo, Judd and Sarah, and even some of the farmers that Mel had visited. Everyone came over to celebrate and just to enjoy being together. Mel handed out drinks and nibbles and chatted with all her new friends. She was thrilled to see Evie enjoying herself too. It was a slower party than maybe they were used to in Melbourne, less of the flashing lights, more sitting outside with a drink of something cool and enjoying the sunshine and conversation, but Evie seemed to be coping.

After the speeches, after Mel had said thank you to the town for accepting her and after her father had said thank you to Graham, Jason, and Bella for the rescue, gradually people wandered back to their own houses and properties and the four of them—Jason, Mr Thompson, Evie, and Mel—were left to tidy up. Not that there was much to do. Dot and Merryn had made themselves at home in the kitchen and that meant continual production of food, and continual washing up.

Finally the four of them sat outside in the warm evening (the weather had been kind for once) and sipped on champagne and whisky and chatted.

'So you think you will be staying here for a while, Mel?'

'Yes, Father, I think that I've finally found the place that suits me. I hope that I can keep going with the Thompsons job for a while if that's OK?'

'Sounds good to me. Maybe we'll expand your reach through Tasmania and you can be our office rep.'

'I love these kind of job interviews, don't you?' Evie said to Jason as an aside.

'You seem to be doing pretty well for yourself in Melbourne now that Tom has gone,' Mel retorted.

'Well, she was the only one who could untangle the mess he had made of the spreadsheets,' said Mel's father.

'Who has the magic skills now?' Mel joshed. And then more seriously, 'How is Senka going?'

'Oh she worked herself out. Turns out she thought Brad was cheating on her but he was just organising a surprise holiday cruise for her.'

'That sounds a bit unstable,' said Jason.

'Yeah, she is a bit, but she's figured that out too and I think she's going to AA now.'

'Well, that's good news. She had us all scared for a minute there.'

'All's well that ends well,' said Mr Thompson and the rest agreed.

'Here's looking forward to some quiet country life now. I'm ready for a rest cure,' said Mel.

'We'll do our best to provide it. I reckon you've earned it,' said Jason, and the rest agreed.

And looking at the bright stars in the night sky, the stress of the months before disappeared into the immensity of the universe and Mel couldn't believe that she had ever been happy anywhere else.

In the end, it had to be said that she was grateful to Angus and, yes, even Slimy Tom, for the reason they gave for her to figure this out. To figure out that life in the country was the life she wanted. Though she hoped never to go through something like that again. She was ready to find out what a quiet country life could bring her. What everyday adventures could be found out here. She was ready to learn to ride a horse, to learn what it took to farm a property, and even to join in with Merryn's knitting group. To adjust her pace of life to suit this absolutely beautiful place. She felt like she had been waiting all her life to move out here and now her new life was ready to start.

And as she snuggled closer to Jason, she knew her new life was going to be beautiful.

Thank you for reading. If you enjoyed this book, please leave a review at your favourite book-buying website to help others find it.

Sign up for my newsletter, and find my other novels and short stories at www.rjamos.com.

Acknowledgements

Right up top I want to thank you Moz for all your encouragement. You have gifted me time to write, and a beautiful place to write, and your confidence in what I am doing is the reason I am able to keep going. Your input as first-reader is invaluable. Thank you, Babe, for everything.

Mum and Dad, my cheer squad and my sales team. Thank you so much for weekly coffees, for your support, and for your joy in my journey.

Chloe, thank you for reading and checking the horse bits, the dog bits, and the general country vibe. From this city girl to you, I totally value all you do. You're the best sister-in-law!

Jill, what can I say? Everyone needs a proof-reader and you are mine. Thanks for the picky read and the super-joyful encouragement.

Sheelagh, I so appreciate your editing expertise. Thanks so much for your time and professionalism.

Father God, this is for you. May it bring you glory.

And to you, the reader, I hope you've loved this adventure. Thank you for reading. A story needs to be read and I love that you've chosen mine. I hope this is the start of a beautiful relationship.